Homes of the Heart

Homes of the Heart
A Ramallah Chronicle

by Farouq Wadi

translated by Dina Bosio and Christopher Tingley

Interlink Books

An imprint of Interlink Publishing Group, Inc.
Northampton, Massachusetts

To Saif

First published in 2007 by

INTERLINK BOOKS
An imprint of Interlink Publishing Group, Inc
46 Crosby Street, Northampton, Massachusetts 01060
www.interlinkbooks.com

Text copyright © Farouq Wadi, 1997, 2007
Translation copyright © Salma Khadra Jayyusi, 2007

Library of Congress Cataloging-in-Publication Data
Wadi, Faruq.
[Manazil al-qalb. English]
Homes of the heart : a Ramallah chronicle / by Farouq Wadi ; translated by Dina Bosio and Christopher Tingley.
p. cm.
ISBN 1-56656-662-2 (pbk.); ISBN 13: 978-1-56656-662-9
1. Ram Allah—Fiction. I. Bosio, Dina. II. Tingley, Christopher. III. Title.
PJ7870.A356M3613 2006
892.7'36—dc22

2006015546

A PROTA Book. This English translation is published with the cooperation of PROTA, (the Project of Translation from Arabic); director: Salma K. Jayyusi, Cambridge, Massachusetts, USA.

Cover image "Orange Picking" by Araf Arafat, courtesy of The Royal Society of Fine Arts, Jordan National Gallery of Fine Art, Amman, Jordan

Printed and bound in the United States of America

Old abodes, you've secure places in the heart
Though barren ground now,
You'll lodge in the heart forever.
—*Al-Mutanabbi*

All longing that's stilled by union is not trustworthy.
—*Ibn 'Arabi*[1]

⁓ 1 ⁓

I was going, at long last, to enter the town and roam its streets. I was going to do the impossible. I was finally walking away from the text, with all its transparent dream and white lies.[2]

And here I was—though I hadn't realized it beforehand—complying with all the rules for entry, rules that wiped out all those roads engraved in my memory: roads that could never have taken me to Ramallah before I'd first gained a glimpse of Jerusalem, with its gold and silver domes, and the sunlight dancing on its walls and markets and graveyards.

Before I'd even dared think I was near Jerusalem, the car had turned to take the road around the city walls with their seven gates. A road that wound its way around my memory too, and was in no hurry to take me to the end of my journey.

Suddenly, there I was in Qalandia. Not a trace was left of Jerusalem. My heart, recognizing the place, beat faster. To my right was the camp, to my left the flickering lights of the runway.

It was there, for the first time, that I'd sensed what traveling was. Joy had swept through me as the twin-engine plane lifted my small body, which felt lighter than ever as the plane moved through space. It was as though my joy then had been no more than a trap, ready to swallow me up as traveling became, in due course, not a matter of delight but my destiny.

In Beirut, I remember, I spent a number of nights trying to summon up images of the Qalandia camp and airport. And when, at last, I succeeded, I began to set down the first lines of my story. In fact I had never lived there, as I claimed, but I needed a setting for the story, somewhere between Ramallah and Jerusalem.

The place stood there still, only now it was rather closer to Ramallah. Jerusalem seemed to have been left behind. The road, full of holes and stones now, made it quite clear it would lead me neither to open blue sky nor to the side of the sea.

A Palestinian policeman met me at the bridge, and I asked him whether he found any problem working with them.

"We don't work with them," he answered briefly. "We work for them."

Amid my mixed feelings, of losing Jerusalem and longing for Ramallah, I tried to chat with the taxi driver. Perhaps he might share some of my sorrows and joys.

"Since when," I asked, "have we got to Qalandia without passing through Jerusalem?"

"Since they opened this road," he said sarcastically, without giving any date. "We follow the roads they map out for us," he added sadly. "It's been that way for a long time now."

With them. For them. We travel to our cities on roads they've built for us.

I'd spent my whole life traveling and writing, and now, suddenly, I'd met a taxi driver who showed me how to read maps and a policeman who corrected my language!

The moment we passed through al-Bireh, twin town to Ramallah, leaving the *arak* factory behind us, I had a sense of floating outside my body, of becoming light as air. The moment had turned me to some transparent substance, as if in a dream. The place around me looked like a dream itself.

Usually, when we're dreaming, we're not surprised when places look different from their real selves; we find ourselves, for the most part, accepting the various changes. Only when we finally wake do we realize how different those dreams were.

Feeling calm and submissive now, I didn't even bother to ask about the savage attack that had destroyed the tranquility of the place taking its name from the open space, and Sat-h Marhaba[3] welcomes you at the entrance to Ramallah. I didn't ask where the gate of al-Bireh New School had gone, the gate that my feet had passed through thousands of times. All I knew was, it had been standing there when I left, in that street that looked narrower and shorter now, and far older even than before. I put no further questions till the car came to a stop in 'Ain Misbah Street, near the lighthouse.

Here I was at the lighthouse—which didn't have any lights. I was in the heart of Ramallah; and yet the town was without heart. No one, no one at all, came to embrace me. No hands waved to me. No one called out my name.

People, crowds, ashes. Yet, no one.

Lost for more than a quarter of a century, I strove to summon up images of the old place. There were no loved ones now, no friends among the crowds. So many people, moving, walking, but no one to keep me company, or lessen my sense of not belonging.

To add to my confusion, and my mingled happiness and shock, everything seemed to merge within the gray night: the traffic, the ugly building, the slogans in their poor handwriting. The new buildings, bereft of all architectural taste, reared up alongside the old, abandoned houses. All the hateful features combined, at that moment, to make me fall out of love with the place I'd dreamed of for so long.

God! How had the town grown so old? How had it lost its memory, withholding from its son all warmth of welcome? Why had we fled from our exiles? Was it just to return to a homeland so like the exile itself?

For those living in exile, and hearing the name Ramallah, it was the lighthouse that first sprang to their minds: that brick structure that rose high in all memory of the town. Crowned with lanterns, it stood in the midst of a round pool, surrounded by greenery and roses, and at its base were four lions' heads with water gushing from the mouths. The whole was surrounded by a circular tarmac path, where people could walk and gaze at the lighthouse and its lions.

The older people of Ramallah, youngsters then, still remembered that day in 1923 when the lighthouse was built. It was those funds sent from America by Ramallah emigrants that had helped build it. No one, though, ever knew where the notion of a lighthouse had sprung from. Lighthouses were usually built, weren't they, in towns with seaports? No one knew why one should have been built in a town that was 25 miles from the sea, and 900 meters above sea level. Did Ramallah, I wondered, sleep and wake to the sound of waves?

Ramallah is built on seven mountains, all facing the sea. When I was a child, the blue sea had gazed at me from afar, as if surrounded by a fence. I was just a kid then, and I believed the myth that the sea was coming closer. I'd run to all the hills, behind the Carlton Hotel near Um Sharayet spring, from the hill of Massyoun to the forest of Batin al-Hawa, where the sea breeze swept in the aroma of cocoa. I'd run, trying to touch the blue sea.

Some of the children would swear they could see the ships in the captive harbors. Mostly, though, we could catch no glimpse of that blue sea, and we'd always blame the fog and mist, or else the dusk.

When, in 1927, an earthquake struck Ramallah, the bell of the Latin Church fell, killing a boy unlucky enough to be just in that spot. A lot of houses were damaged, and walls fell. And all the while the lighthouse stood firm.

In the 1950s, the Lighthouse Square was open to all the political parties of the time, the meeting point for the crowds of people streaming out of the two towns. There it was that the Communist and Ba'ath parties, who dominated the political arena then, confronted one another. People would gather to shout slogans calling for the downfall of the Baghdad Pact, or to denounce the attack on the Suez Canal—though they were one in hailing Egypt's Gamal Abd al-Nasser and Arab unity. Often enough the Lighthouse Square turned into a battlefield between demonstrators and soldiers. Control of the lighthouse by the army and the Bedouin security forces meant control of the two towns and a curfew enforced.

On my right was the Salah Pharmacy. The name could still be read on the sign hanging from the roof of the building: that same roof where, long ago, people would stand if they wanted to make a speech—there, or else on the small balcony on the opposite side of the building, facing the other side of the Lighthouse Square, that scene of a great and bygone political era.

That same balcony, where a sign with a doctor's name hung now, had once rung with the voices of Abdullah al-Rimawi, Hamdi al-Taji al-Farouqi, and Kamal Nasser, all of whom had run in the Jordanian elections under the banner of the Ba'ath Party. On that balcony, too, had stood Fayeq Warrad, the first Palestinian Communist ever to win a seat in the Jordanian Parliament, together with the Communist doctor Yaqoub Ziyadin, who came from the Jordanian village of As-Sammakiya, near al-Karak, and who'd been resoundingly elected as the representative for Jerusalem. The leaders of the National Movement had no loudspeakers then. Yet how strong and splendid their voices had been, and how very clear!

This balcony seemed far smaller than before, and not as high as it seemed then. Could it really have grown smaller and lower? Or had our bodies, defying the defeat and the heavy burdens, become taller—so much taller that we could reach up now and touch the doctor's sign?

Back in the mid-1960s, I'd stood for long hours, among crowds that filled the roads and roofs, waiting for President Bourguiba's parade to pass through the town on its way from Nablus to Jerusalem. The crowds had gathered to denounce the Tunisian president's declarations, which were viewed as an outrageous call for betrayal. He'd called for a peace initiative that would satisfy both parties, Arab and Israeli, one based on international law and recognition of the Israeli entity, which was then regarded as illegal. The crowds shouted for two or three minutes as the parade passed by. The president, though, paid no attention, not even bothering to look at the people.

Twenty years later, in 1987, I was one of the Palestinian journalists the Tunisian president invited to his palace in Carthage. He reminded us of his former initiative, which the PLO had then viewed as downright treason, but which was in fact (as he noted) quite close to the PLO's present stance. Older by then, with a good deal of distorted wisdom, we gave the president a round of applause.

Where had the lighthouse gone? And those people we'd loved so much, who'd stood on the balcony and the roof of Salah Pharmacy? Where were they now?

～ 2 ～

So here I was, carrying my small bag, walking the streets of a town that had failed to recognize me, after I'd been away for a quarter of a century that felt more like a lifetime.

I crossed al-Mughtaribreen (Expatriates') Square, which looked smaller and remoter than ever. It had been turned into a car park with concrete complexes at the corners, one of them replacing Naoum Park, where people had once enjoyed the smell of grilled meat and *arak*. The place was called Clock Square now.

Leaving this behind me, I took the road to Ramallah Park, and found myself reminiscing over every inch of a place that had long held a place in my heart. It was, I was positive, only the old, deeply worn asphalt that allowed me to retrace the long-forgotten route.

Now, for the first time, my heart started beating joyfully, as I approached al-Bardawni: the place where, one summer night with a friend called Raheef, I discovered the pleasure of drinking *arak* and listened to al-Sayyab's poem about the rain.[4] After a while I passed by the girls' school where someone's heart there knew the beat of love for me, and where my initials were cut into an old wooden desk.

As my heart happily wandered the place, I stumbled across a small hotel that had somehow survived, amid the ruins of other old summer hotels that had once nestled peacefully in the arms of the evergreen pines.

I left my bag there, then hurried out into the streets before night fell, in search of what had once been mine. But even the streets, I found, had fled, leaving only their ashes on the sidewalks.

The police station that had once stood between al-Mughtaribreen Square and the town's main street wasn't there any more. In its place was a new commercial center. The old asphalt road was a sea of pebbles now, just for pedestrians and the vendors who spread out their goods by the sides of the road. I entered this main street, peopled by its concrete ghosts. How small I felt, walking among those tall buildings, which simply didn't fit in with a the narrow place, to say nothing of its outrageous violation of the town's indigenous architecture.

One place only looked to have struggled hard for its existence and solitude, and that was the small old house with the rose bush, standing firm on one of the corners, where people had once enjoyed the tasty food of al-Kurdi Restaurant (as it then was).

The roses were the only change for the better. It was amusing, though, to see a coffee shop (originally a shoe shop) called "It Was Bata Once." Likewise, Abd al-Nour Bookshop near the Meeting House of the Friends' Mission, which was my only source for oil colors, had gone and given the place to a falafel restaurant.

A lot of places, despite all the changes, had kept the same names and sites: the famous Rukab Ice Cream, for instance, although it had lost its summer garden to one of those huge buildings. As for the Abu Iskandar Restaurant, the only change I could see was that its fat owner who had given his name to the place, and to its tasty pastries, wasn't there any more.

A few yards ahead I could see the Dunya Cinema, sadly decrepit now. It was there where I watched Brigitte Bardot stripping for just three piasters,[5] which I held tight in my hand because my pockets were full of holes.

On the other side of al-Manara Square, where the main street ran on to al-Nahda Street coming from al-Bireh, stood al-Walid Cinema. Here it was that Said Mahran was shot seven times—the number of times I saw the film of *The Thief and the Dogs*.[6] I always hoped he'd escape the police bullets, but he let me down every time!

This place, which had supplied us with pictures and fed our imaginations for just three piasters, was in ruins too; it had been engulfed in darkness for seven long years. When I revisited the place two years later, there were once more posters for a film, and one thoroughly worthy of al-Walid Cinema's return. It was called *Nasser '56*.

A few yards on from there, I saw to my amazement that the sign for the al-Ilmiyya Bookshop, produced in the 1950s by the famous calligrapher Jinho, was still hanging there. Jinho had been the dominant figure, then, for the signs in both towns. None of the young calligraphers (who included my brother, Ali) could compete with Jinho's Persian characters and vibrant colors. Not even Muhammad Siyam, master calligrapher and chief teacher in Palestine and Jordan, renowned as the master of black ink and Thuluth calligraphy—even he couldn't match Jinho's practical skills.

Al-Ilmiyya Bookshop had also stayed faithful to its address too: PO Box 64, telephone number 64—even if phone numbers did have seven digits now. The memory of this bookshop was apparently stuck in the 1950s.

The playground of the Hashemite School was gone, to make room for more offices and clinics, taking with it the echo of my steps where I'd once chased after a soccer ball. (Its old glamour can only be saved by turning the old school premises into a cultural center.)

Alongside the school had once been the Health Department, which had issued my birth certificate, old and torn now (though this hardly mattered to those who'd spent their lives in exile, and whose time had passed by). Here it was that my eyes had stung from drops and my cuts from iodine. Now, I saw, to my consternation, that the place had been turned into an Israeli military post. There were soldiers everywhere, on the roof and around every corner, pointing their weapons at the streets and sidewalks, at tranquility itself. Their eyes were on the lookout for any slight movement in the darkness that was now sinking to envelope me. As I stood there, cold and alone, it was as though those drops and that iodine were coursing to sting my heart.

I was longing to know what had become of the Friends' School nearby, but found myself retreating in the face of a machine gun ready to target anything that moved, amid a darkness of which I already formed part.

Feeling flat and depressed, I walked beneath the dim lights, in the teeth of a strong wind that insistently turned the windmills of my memory. And so I returned, to spend my first night utterly alone and in a freezing cold bed. That was all I could get from the town where I'd been born, and where I'd spent my childhood and youth—the very town I'd written about for so long from my exile, with such ceaseless love and longing.

~ 3 ~

When I checked into the small hotel, I'd found an old issue of an Arabic newspaper, which I borrowed, hoping it would help me sleep. It wasn't long, though, before I found myself looking for something else to read. The only thing I could find, unfortunately, was my own novel, in which I'd written about my town and my childhood. I put it to one side, being one who finds no interest in reading their own books. Or perhaps I might have found many of the events I'd set down upsetting.

But sleeplessness drew me back to all these ill-starred things, and I passed the night reading what my dreams and longings had once made me write down. Had it not been for the night, and the occupation troops patrolling the place, I would have acted on my powerful urge to put the book down, go out of the room, and rediscover the place. As it was, I had no option but to spend that first night reading my own book, into the early hours.

Next morning, I crossed al-Mughtaribreen Square and al-Manara Square, without any hostile feelings toward them. I walked along Broadcasting Street (which older people liked to call "Radio Street" and the young "Lovers' Road").

What I saw gave me a nasty shock. The tall trees so alive in my memory were gone, replaced by those vast buildings. To the right I could see the remains of an abandoned house, looking for the entire world like an old man leaning on his stick, searching for a lost beauty and people long since gone.

This place standing there in the wilderness had once been known as the Harb Hotel, and, many years before, two beautiful young women had lived opposite it. They belonged to an older generation than mine, and I didn't even dare dream about them. But those older than I were infatuated with their beauty—like my brother, who named a daughter after one of them.

Even in exile, the beauty of these two women remained a live subject. One of them, so it was said, had married an Arab prince from the Gulf. Then, when she'd grown tired of living cooped up inside his palace, she'd regained her freedom, gone off to Paris, and there married an aristocratic Frenchman, who'd been unable to find any woman more beautiful in the whole of France!

Radio Street had managed to keep some of its old features, despite all the construction, which made it look smaller than before and not so green. By contrast, al-Hamra Palace Hotel, with its old brick roof, hadn't escaped the gloomy changes, though its transformation to a dormitory for women students had done something at least to save it from the ravages and turmoil of the times.

Next to the hotel was a huge building put up during the British mandate, in the second half of the 1920s, to serve as a headquarters for the British Military Administration. Over the next three decades, that same building had been used by the Jordanians, the Israelis, and finally by the Palestinian Authority. Originally known just as the "Center," it became the "Israeli Military Administration Center," with the word "Civil" added subsequently. Nowadays people called it the "Governorate."

Whatever the passing events and various names, the building always kept a very special meaning for me. One rainy night long ago, some months after my family had fled their village of al-Muzairia'a and taken refuge in a tent in the yard behind the Center, the cry of a newborn baby pierced the silence. That child, so I learned later, was none other than me!

My father, who loved to make up stories, didn't think twice about fabricating an account he hoped would amuse the family, but the fact is it haunted me forever after. They had, he claimed, found me close by the tent at a place where nomadic gypsies used to pitch their tents, covered in mud and sucking my fingers in my hunger. So they'd decided, he went on, to take me in and feed me, and in the end they'd kept me. Why not? After all, I was dark and had black eyes, just like them!

From the moment I heard that story, terror would strike me whenever the gypsies passed through our quarter. It was the sharp look in those eyes of theirs, as though searching for something long lost, and their dark skin. I went into hiding whenever they came by.

It wasn't easy for me to catch a glimpse into the yard of the very place I was born in, because of the heavily armed occupation forces, along with the wire fences and the searchlights that were switched on night and day.

The first home I ever knew—apart, that is, from my mother's womb and the tent where I was born—was a room in the Center, which the officers had given my family after my birth, and because my condition was worsening. The officers had suggested to my father that he might name me Abdullah, after the King of Transjordan, but my father insisted on calling me Farouq after the then–King of Egypt—something he regretted he'd ever done when President Gamal Abd al-Nasser came to dominate the Arab political arena. So it was that my family at last got a roof over their heads, after the many hard months living in a tent.

One day I accompanied my mother who went to visit a friend who'd just married an officer and was living in one of the rooms of the Center. And my mother told me: "That's where they put us to live when you were born."

My family often talked of that night we first moved to the room, and of how my brother, Mahmoud, looked out of the window and said: "God help those refugees! How can they stand it, living in tents like that?"

It was there, in the yard at the back of the Center, that my brothers had their first taste of work, selling candies and sesame cakes and cleaning shoes. I was lucky. As the youngest of the family, I was spared from working, and spared, too, from wearing those formal gray jackets a genius tailor in Ramallah had discovered a way to make from old, gray blankets.

As I grew up, I twice visited the Center. The first time was when I went, along with my father, to visit my brother Zuhair, who'd been arrested for taking part in a demonstration in support of Gamal Abd al-Nasser and Arab Unity (later, of course, he became wise enough to forget all about such protests). The second time was when Abul Hafez, the principal of Ramallah High School, had me take a copy of the student magazine, which I and some fellow students wanted to bring out, and give it to the frightening intelligence officer, Mr. Arnaki, to censor before it was published. It was no joke publishing a magazine in those days!

The copy of the magazine never left the Center. We knocked on every door, trying to find what had become of it, but we were turned away, sometimes politely, sometimes rudely. In the end we gave the whole thing up, and the magazine was never published again.

Now, though, I could look out onto the yard of the place I was born in from any northern window of the Palestinian Ministry of Culture, which was next door to the Center. The yard had been covered in tarmac ready for the visit of the French President, and this buried what remained of the green grass that had, for so long, witnessed the clubs and arms of the occupation forces.

From a distance the Center seemed to be painted white, and a concrete wall had replaced the ugly walls of sandbags. Oddly enough, a natal clinic had been built in the yard at the back!

Whenever I recalled the Center in my exile, I'd smell the dung of the horses and hear them neighing, and hear the barking of the trained police dogs. And I'd dream I might get back the copy of that confiscated magazine.

∼ 4 ∼

Ramallah, twin town to al-Bireh, is set on hills over-looking the blue sea and best known for its vast expanse of vineyards.

Two towns and yet one town. The last refuge, opening its gates and spreading its green grass to welcome wanderers such as Rashed bin Saqer al-Haddadeen and Hussein al-Banaweyeh, who arrived in the sixteenth century from the eastern bank of the river Jordan, and that obscure policeman who came to the town half a century ago, along with so many other refugees uprooted from Lydd, Ramleh, and Jaffa after the great defeat; and, finally, myself, just returned from my exile. The town was home and refuge for those who'd lost both.

I sent my mind back to that time when the warrior had been transformed to policeman. I'd been born in this town, after the great tragedy that had struck its people, and after years of armed struggle. The man who'd learned to make mines, who'd fought with the first guerrilla group under Hasan Salameh, was a policeman now, guarding the radio station, watching over Ramallah's Communists and Ba'athists and helping direct the traffic.

Does history really repeat itself, I wondered, once as tragedy and once as comedy? And just where, I asked myself, did tragedy end and comedy begin?

The image of the thin, short policeman who'd spur people on to demonstrate, who'd spend the nights playing cards at the homes of Communists he was supposed to be watching, was stored in the memory of Ramallah's streets. He was questioned once over the part he'd played in urging on demonstrators to burn down the British Council, at the time of the attack on the Suez Canal. And he was arrested too, one cold night, when he was seen waving his leg instead of his arm, for cars to pass. As bad luck would have it, the district commander had chosen just that moment to drive by.

"Are you blind?" shouted the commander furiously.

"Yes," rejoined the policeman, "and deaf too, sir."

He'd stand near the windmill (now replaced by a building), at the small roundabout (gone now), and there he'd signal for cars to move on and salute the people passing by. He gave the impression the roads were flowing out from his frail body. Even the small roundabout looked as if it had been specially tailored for him.

The first of the roads leading out from the roundabout went to Ash-Shurfa Quarter, which in turn led on to Jerusalem. The second road was An-Nahda Street, which led to al-Manara Square, before leading on to the Balou' district on the way to Nablus. The fourth road was an extension of the Jerusalem road and led to the Paradise Quarter.

That thin, short policeman was my father, who spent sixteen years serving in the Jordanian police force. He was the reverse of serious or disciplined, which was why he was never decorated with any badge. Not that he cared very much, because he never thought those badges would do anything to save us from poverty. As for my mother, she'd learned over the years to ask him the same question at the end of every month: "How much have they taken off your salary?"

The only time I ever saw my father act seriously was when my eldest brother, Suleiman, joined the armed forces and came back home in his uniform. I remember seeing my father stand and salute the young officer who'd just walked in.

Then, the very next morning, as he stood in line with some of the other policemen, he heard the corporal say:

"Take a step—back!"

"Take a step back?" shouted my father angrily. "How much further back are you going? Will you not go forward one day?"

The corporal decided my father had gone too far.

"Watch your tongue, policeman!" he yelled. "Or you'll be up before a court martial!"

By now the thin policeman had lost his temper completely.

"Don't you threaten me, corporal!" he yelled back. "Do you not realize that what's here between my legs produced an officer in your army?" (The words he actually used are too rude to be written down.)

The corporal and the other policemen burst out laughing. If they hadn't my father would have come home to my mother at the end of the month and told her the whole of his salary had been deducted as punishment!

So, the thin policeman was my father, and it was at Ras al-Tahouna that I knew what I might call my first home, excluding the tent and the temporary room at the Center. There it was that my early childhood memories of a home, a quarter, and a nursery school would be born.

— 5 —

I'd returned to the cradle of my childhood, to the spring of my memories and source of my early dreams. I was recalling the scattered memories I'd conjured up so vividly in my book.

In all the years I lived there, I never knew the place was called Ras al-Tahouna. I'd called it the Paradise Quarter, a name stemming, clearly, from the strong sense of loss and the ceaseless dreams of one day returning home. I didn't mean to mislead when I replaced Tahouna [windmill] with Paradise. No doubt the change simply sprang from the wish to reveal a deep underlying truth. The real name was less poetic, and yet the place itself never lost its allure, not deep down in my heart, where some constant, drowsy sense awakened all the feelings that had slept so soundly in my blood.

A famous Arab poet once said: "Many homes a man knows; yet he will always long for the first." And the philosopher Gaston Bachelard had to write an entire book, *La Poétique de l'espace* [The Poetics of Space], to explore and prove this notion.

The echo of the Arab poet's words could be heard in the narrow alley that led to an old brick house resting amid an orchard of almond and plum trees. The house had a clear, open look, just as it had always appeared in my memory. Seeing it was like watching a vision from a book spring to life.

With fingers that shook, tentative and awe-struck, I knocked on the door of my first brick home. My eyes searched for one particular almond tree, which had played a tragic role in my life and writing alike. It was forty years before that I'd fallen from that tree, and body and memory had borne the scars ever since.

It was without malice that I turned to gaze at the broken trunk that was all that remained, and it was as though the trunk was gazing back at me, regretting the pain it had caused me once. In my book I'd forgiven it. My heart had no room left for pain and hatred, especially toward a tree that had once given me almonds, shade, and a strong branch to hang my swing from.

Abu Ali and Umm Ali, who still lived in the house, didn't welcome me as they would have welcomed just any tenant led home by feelings of nostalgia. They were overjoyed to recapture a part of the place that had been lost for so long. It seemed, indeed, as though they were clinging on to all those lost times, striving to rid themselves—for a short while at least—of their isolation and the alien, forsaken feelings it brought.

They weren't like just any landlords, any more than we'd

been just ordinary tenants. We'd all lived together, with no barriers. We'd exchange homes if ever there was need for more space. It took only a few minutes, and no great physical effort, to move what furniture there was.

The house had two doors, one to the north and one to the south, which meant that each family had its own entrance. Our part of the house had comprised two small rooms, and there was a door separating our small section from their much bigger quarters, which in fact we often occupied. The small kitchen was divided into two equal parts by a thin wooden board, which my brother Ali, the family artist, decorated with a butterfly in colored chalk. If ever Umm Ali and my mother wanted to borrow some coffee or sugar from one another, they'd remove this board, and, little by little, the touch of their hands rubbed out the butterfly. There was no need, though, to remove the board when they wanted to gossip or exchange recipes. Only our dreams were free to float and wander, without any need for permission from the sleepers in the two homes.

The place seemed smaller than I remembered it. The walls of the room looked much closer together, and the corridor where we'd once played soccer now barely had space for my feet, swollen by the roads of exile.

What most worried Umm Ali, though, was very different from what concerned me.

"Just imagine, there were sixteen of us in this house once, and now Abu Ali and I are the only two left."

I went for a walk in the orchard with Abu Ali. We moved toward the trunk of the almond tree.

"Look!" Abu Ali said. "That's all there is left of the

almond tree where you hurt yourself. We had it cut down. It was ill-omened."

He went on to talk about the accident, and the evil results that had stayed with me from the time I was a child till now, when the white hair had come to invade my head, threatening what was left of my days and spirit. He recalled how no one, anywhere in the quarter, had been expert enough to mend the bone in my left arm, which broke when I fell from the almond tree. He'd carried me on his back, like a horse, till he found a car to take us to Deir Dabwan, where the folk doctor specialized in bone fractures. Without of course meaning to, the doctor only made things worse. I ended up with a paralyzed arm, which I changed to an amputated leg in my book.

And now here was this man taking me back to see the orchard and its plum trees, taking pains to restore, within his memory, the aging bones he could feel cracking and fading away in his own body. He pointed to the houses still somehow staying upright, and sighed.

"The place hasn't changed," he said. "It's just time that's moved on! You all left, and we stayed behind. None of the people we knew then stayed in those houses. The world changed, and the people changed with it. Nowadays no one knows anyone. No one knocks on anyone's door. Where have the old times gone? Where have the people gone? Where are they?"

He began recalling the people who'd lived in the quarter once, and who still lived on in his heart, in his spirit and memory. He talked of them as if he could see them still, with his old, tired eyes. They kept on wandering through his memory, which had no power to stop them returning.

All those men and women and children, who lived there in

his heart, in his very bones, came back. All the big events and little incidents, only waiting, you would have thought, for me to return, came pouring, flooding out of a memory still clinging to a time long gone, a time that would never come back.

How ironic it was! I'd returned, to find a man who'd never left the place I'd come searching for. All that concerned him was the passing of time.

How even more ironic it was! The man who kept the place and its people alive in his heart and in his bones, died of bone cancer just a few months after my visit. Then I returned only once more to my childhood home—this time to tender my condolences to Umm Ali, the woman now still more forsaken and plunged in loneliness, in a home where once sixteen people had lived.

— 6 —

I stood in the square that I'd called Paradise Square in my book. It was divided into two streets now, and looked a lot smaller. Still, though, it had a quiet, tranquil feel, which was just what my spirit needed. I crossed the frontier of time, and heard once more the footsteps of those who'd passed by the square so long ago. I myself had been one of them.

My steps were a young man's steps then, my way strewn with roses. Now my steps were as old as I was, as weary and broken as my spirit itself.

The people I'd loved were long gone, some turned to ashes, some still in their distant exiles. I turned back to the "Paradise" of my text. It still seemed like paradise to me. For all the long autumn that had engulfed the place, for all the loneliness and loss.

In this square Karawan had once sold the children ice cream. He could tell the exact time by looking at the sun. The magic box[7] (*sundouq al-'ajab*) would come through the square too, with its splendid colors and wondrous pictures of shining knights. And here would come Abul Deeb, during the harvest time of green chickpeas, and of Indian figs whose thorns never once managed to prick his fingers.

Gypsies would come to sell their ironware, and musicians would pass through the square too, on their way to the radio station, hurrying on as the children pursued them and begged them to play some music or sing a song. The Green Man with the fiery eyes, who got his name from the green outfit he always wore, would set up at the square and sharpen knives. When he stopped coming, the rumor spread that he'd last been spotted crossing the no-man's zone into Palestine. Some evil people said he hadn't gone back to Palestine out of love, but because he was a spy for Israel!

The quinine trees, which had long abandoned the place in my book, were gone in reality now, all but one solitary tree. I couldn't even find any remains of the trunks of the lost trees. Could it be the trees had grown tired of their solitude too, in the forsaken square, and chosen to leave forever? And could it be that my imagination doubled their number in my book, just as it lengthened their branches and multiplied the number of their leaves?

I halted by the steps of my first nursery school, the Adla al-Akkad kindergarten, and recalled the stern but kind lady with the glass eye, who always smelled of shiny colored paper. The kindergarten occupied three back rooms at the back of the ground floor of the building set up on probably the highest hill of the two towns. The mayor of al-Bireh at the time, Abdallah al-Jawdah, who was also the landlord, used to live there. There too lived the teacher, Salameh Khalil, with his wife Samiha Khalil, who would later set up her society, Ina'ash al-Usrah [Family Welfare], which was to become a major landmark of the town.

I stood there for a long time by the steps, amazed at how in my book I'd portrayed them as "long and broad." I tried measuring and counting them, and found they were actually far smaller than I'd imagined and set down in words.

On the left side of the road, before reaching the steps, lay a small alley leading to a house. More important, though, than the house itself was the opening I found on the right side of the alley. It was half covered by rubble, of course, but I could still make out the cave that lay beneath the hill and the building.

When we were children, we'd stand at the entrance to the cave, frightened by the darkness and by all the rumors we'd heard about the place.

"This cave," one of us would say, "goes all the way through to al-Taweel Mountain."

"It reaches," others would answer, "right to the foot of Karantal Mountain—maybe to the Dead Sea even!"

We used to say the path through the cave was full of old ruins and marble columns, part of a palace of long ago. It was always an eerie feeling, standing by the entrance to that cave— a place liable to turn the hair of nervous people white.

No one dared go inside, even a few steps. In all truth, I believe the cave went no deeper than a few yards in from the entrance.

I made an effort to remember all the rumors, which seemed to have come from the unknown. Recently I'd learned that Ras al-Tahouna had been inhabited since the Bronze Age;

in the past few years they'd found some pottery and swords dating back to that ancient period of human history. Was our cave one of the places where those objects had been found? Objects that would dispel the illusions of the children of the Paradise Quarter?

All the time I'd lived in my exile, plunged deep in longing for the place, I'd never known that Ras al-Tahouna, so tranquil and green in my memory and my books alike, had been the scene of two historic battles. The first had been when the Palestinian revolutionaries faced the army of Jamal Pasha during his campaign in Syria in 1834. The second had been in 1917, when a force of exhausted Turkish soldiers, trying to defend the remnants of a dying empire, had taken up position in Ras al-Tahouna to fight the young, vigorous troops of the British Empire. Thereafter, following a triumph that would cast its shadow over our history, and profoundly affect our experience throughout the twentieth century, our country had become subject to the British mandate.

The clever Mrs. Adla al-Akkad, whose glass eye hadn't stopped her discovering the beauty of the place, had never told her young pupils about the two battles, even though she'd helped those same pupils, through the site she'd chosen for her nursery school, to develop their budding sense of the geography of heart, soul, and conscience.

— 7 —

*A*s my eyes examined the place, so my memory flashed back to brighten every corner and every stone; these, in their turn, recalled distant events, and people who filled the cracked walls of my vibrant recollection.

I'd gaze at a house, and the people who'd lived there would come surging out. I had only to call the place to mind, and back would come all the departed spirits wandering in their exiles, or in heaven.

In that house over there lived my first friend Issam, who'd go with me each day to Mrs. Adla's nursery school. We wore black uniforms with bleached white collars that hurt our tender necks. His Egyptian mother was named Firdaws, meaning "paradise"—the very name I'd chosen for one of the quarters in my book—and she'd urge the people of the quarter to love Abd al-Nasser. She even tried to make them believe his image appeared on the surface of the moon. "Vote for Fayeq

Warrad!" she'd shout.[8] She was very active and lively, and her beautiful voice was a constant reminder of Abd al-Nasser. I later learned that one of her legs had been amputated due to diabetes. She'd gone to live in the US, where she'd been confined to a wheelchair, and where, with grief and pain, she'd gaze at the summer moon that stubbornly failed to give back Abd al-Nasser's image.

Abd al-Nasser was, beyond all doubt, the chief man of the quarter. No one dared say anything against him, apart from my mother, who accused him of burning her radio, the only item left to the family from their lost homeland.

My brother, Mahmoud, who was nicknamed "the radio" because of his ceaseless yelling and screaming, picked up that radio, and nothing else, from our home that we were to leave forever. He even forgot to take the car battery we used to operate it with.

My father was greatly attached to this radio. It was only the second to have appeared in our village of al-Muzairia'a, and he was careful to get to know about it piece by piece. His skillful fingers and active screwdriver never failed to fix it whenever the need arose.

The only problem was that he knew so much about it that he'd use it as a hiding place in emergencies. During a raid targeting on the homes on the Communists, the Ba'athists, and anything pertaining to the name of Abd al-Nasser, my father, that thin policeman, hid a book called *In Freedom's Name* in the radio. It was a technically poor novel the young Gamal Abd al-Nasser had started writing, and which had later been completed by the author Abd al-Rahim 'Ajjaj, now long forgotten.

The inspectors were looking for any evidence that would help them send an accused person to al-Jafr desert camp, which was spacious enough to accommodate everybody. Luckily they didn't inspect the radio, the hiding place of the policeman who idolized Abd al-Nasser.

Several months passed, and we'd all forgotten about the book and where it had been hidden. Then one morning, smoke started billowing through our home, and through the neighbors' homes too, burning both the radio and the book inside it, along with the Voice of the Arabs,[9] and that of Abd al-Halim Hafez[10]—and turning off the voice of Abd al-Nasser, to which family and neighbors would gather to listen. People then would sit huddled around the radio, so the voice wouldn't be picked up by the hearing devices of the authority that searched for any sound coming from the cracks of those frightened homes.

As for my mother, she stood there, in front of the burned radio and the ashes of the book, "That," she stormed, "is all we've gotten from Gamal Abd al-Nasser!"

A woman had just stepped out to sweep the threshold of the second house that was written on my heart. I wanted to ask if I could go in, but she seemed too busy to answer me. My restless spirit, though, didn't fail me. It was ready enough to find a way into all the locked rooms, making light of the closed windows and the rusty old doors sealed with the red wax of time passing.

I entered the place in my memory, taking no notice of the present time, and all the windows and doors and the new faces, and the old woman's broom that was sweeping her dust and mine from the threshold of the house. I tried to collect my memories.

It was in that room to the right, which I couldn't now enter in the body, that I'd stood one night and for the first time made my avowals of love, and known all the feelings of excitement and confusion they entailed.

Another room here—another room there—a first memory here—and another there.

Behind the iron bars of the window of one of those rooms, I'd spent a whole afternoon with a small girl, our backs glued to the wall as we watched her mother give birth.

This pretty young girl had recently scratched my face with her nails, and we'd both asked our families not to interfere—even if we decided to elope one day. This same girl stood firm that afternoon, insisting on seeing her mother give birth. I had no option but to declare my unflinching support for her. I stood by her side as we shouted together: "We won't leave the room!" The other women there, who included my mother, gave up on us. The midwife, Hajja Thurayya, who helped both our mothers deliver, rushed across, and the steam from the boiling water filled the room.

We stood there watching, our eyes wide and our hearts beating fast, as the other women encouraged the woman in labor. The situation made us act like two good children, and, with the first cry of the newborn baby, the mother's cries ceased and the other women all rejoiced and cried out:

"*Jamil! Jamil!* [Beautiful! Beautiful!]"

And Jamil he was named. No one could know then that he was destined to die young.

Holding hands, we ran like a pair of deer toward the al-Ilmiyya Bookshop, where my friend's father, Uncle Abu Salah, worked, and where he was waiting for the good news amid the books and stationery he was selling. But, to our surprise, we found my sister, Yusra, had beaten us to it, winning the reward my uncle had promised to the one who was first to bring him the good news. Only then did I realize why my father and his fellow policemen called my sister the "black knight."

So the black knight got the great reward, which was half a dinar. As for us, all we got from my uncle, his face beaming with joy, was some paper and colored pencils, along with a pat on the head and a smile.

Abu Salah (Muhammad Hasan Salah) was a man who could laugh till his sides ached, and yet he was, at the same time, so serious he could sit up through long nights deciphering the various ambiguities found in the *Kapital* [of Karl Marx].

He was a person who'd never been mentioned in books, perhaps because he was one of those fighters who worked silently, away from the spotlight.

He'd led the armed band of his village, al-Muzairia'a, being regarded as the most educated among a group which included Muhammad al-Abd Wahdan, Saleh al-Kayed, and Muhammad Ahmad Wadi. Their commander-in-chief, Shaikh Hasan Salameh, named the band the "Vanguard Squadron," which was a source of great pride to them all.

During the battle in which Hasan Salameh was killed, Muhammad Salah was hit by a bullet that left his right arm paralyzed till the end of his days.

He was one of the few Communists to evade arrest during the campaign waged in April 1957, following the decision to prohibit political parties and impose martial law throughout the country following the dismissal of the national coalition government of Suleiman al-Nabulsi. This short-lived government was formed during the political surge that gave the national forces the status of a parliamentary majority.

One dark night in the spring, Muhammad Salah fled Ramallah, eluding all the eyes that were on constant watch for him. He left for Moscow, little knowing he'd never return to Ramallah.

Date: January 22, 1979
Place: Beirut

It would have been just another warm, sunny afternoon in Beirut—had it not been for the vast explosion that rocked the city, shaking my house on Madame Curie Street. The date was to occupy a meaningful place in my memory, which had striven to escape from such sounds.

Next morning, while drinking my coffee and reading the shocking news in the morning paper, I heard a light, almost shy knock on my door. When I opened I found in front of me Muhammad Hasan Salah, the comrade of Hasan Salameh, gazing at me, the tears welling in his defeated eyes.

The explosion had targeted the handsome Palestinian security officer, Ali Hasan Salameh, killing him along with a number of his comrades. One of these had been Jamil Muhammad Salah.

A few hours later I was standing alongside Uncle Muhammad Salah in the Martyrs' Cemetery, gazing at the grave freshly dug to receive the dead body. It was wrapped in a red flag and covered with red roses, symbol of the lost youth of a young man who'd always been in a hurry, as if rushing to keep an appointment. There he was, leaving us so prematurely, as if he had an early appointment with death itself.

As they flung the earth onto the dead body, I uttered a cry like the one I heard, years before, let out by a newborn child at his birth: a child swiftly emerging to walk the paths of life that would lead him to this tragic end.

In the house where condolences were tendered, Muhammad Salah sat listening to Yasser Arafat as he told how Shaikh Hasan Salameh had died in action, seeking a parallel between the deaths of the father and the son. Muhammad Salah, who'd taken part in that battle, didn't try to raise his paralyzed arm to tell Yasser Arafat he'd actually been there. He made no effort to correct or support anything of what was said. He remained silent, listening to the account of the historic event as though he'd taken no part in it. He didn't point out the difference involved: that when Hasan Salameh had died, he'd been left alive, while the son, Ali Hasan Salameh, had made sure to take Jamil with him on his final journey.

That man's silence, his remarkable gift for listening, made him an ideal fighter at a time when the struggle had turned to a sad, tedious affair of words.

~ 8 ~

*D*uring the 1956 elections, support in my quarter was divided between the Communist and Ba'ath parties. The latter, though, was the stronger, since this was the prime period of Arab Nationalism. The ideology of communism was under constant attack as well as its notions of class struggle, religion and sex. That of class struggle was looked at as a prescription for bloodbaths, that of religion meant atheism, and that of sex meant licentiousness. As for Abd al-Nasser, there was never any dispute over him.

My family had decided to support the Ba'ath Party for various and cogent reasons. Abdullah al-Rimawi was a distant friend of the family; Hamdi al-Taji al-Farouqi was the family doctor. As for Kamal Nasser, the fact that he was a poet was enough. My brother Ismail, the poet in our family, urged everyone to vote for poetry and the Ba'ath party together.

On the nights before any demonstration, against the

Baghdad Pact, or on any other issue, people would gather in secret (as they supposed), by the light of lanterns, and watch my brother Ali, the calligrapher, write the slogans that, the next morning, would be held aloft and loudly chanted through the town.

During the hours of curfew that mostly followed these demonstrations (the demonstrations themselves ended, invariably, under the total control of the army and the Bedouin forces brought to the town), the quarter would have an air of unity and support among its people, who'd visit one another and exchange food and rumors. As for my brother, he'd return to his oil paints, sitting under the almond tree and producing pictures of rivers and mermaids on what was left of the boards he'd used to write slogans.

I was amazed at the smallness of the area once occupied by the small bakery (long since destroyed, the rubble remaining there for a long time before it was finally removed) on one of the corners of the town square. This small area had been hugely magnified in my book—to the extent that Hamad al-Taweel, an emigrant who returned from America, had wanted to build a seven-story building with elevators (they called them electric boxes) that carry people upwards to a shopping center staffed by young women in mini-skirts.

I'd enjoyed what I thought was an attractive lie I created in my book, quite intentionally forgetting that the Paradise Quarter could never accommodate a building on that scale. And yet—to my amazement—there was now a building, of much the same size and type, being put up very near the site I'd envisaged!

I asked the building workers a few questions about it. "It's a building with seven floors," they replied.

Would I be able to rent an apartment there? I asked. No, they said, it was to be a commercial center, just shops and offices. And it would have elevators!

The real shock, though, came when I asked who the owner was. One of the workmen said:

"It belongs to someone from the al-Taweel family."

When I wrote my book, I never realized a family called al-Taweel existed in the village. Could the name have been lodged in my subconscious, ready to surface at the right moment? I thought of the formula writers use at the start of a book: "All the characters and events in this book are fictitious."

At any rate, I was spurred on to examine the family trees for al-Bireh village. All the families, I discovered, had sprung from six main families, who, back in the nineteenth century, had formed a military unit calling itself "al-Bireh Brigade." Its members were from the families of al-Kuraan, al-Rafidi, al-Hamayel, al-Aabed, al-Karakrah—and al-Taweel.

~ 9 ~

*I*n my book I called the man Rayan al-Taweel, and he'd come to the Paradise Quarter to turn the stones of the demolished bakery into tombstones and crosses, which he engraved with his magical hands and transformed into living witnesses, beautiful and magnificent.

I went in search of the old man I'd recalled, from actual memory, when I created this character: a man who used to be found on the corner, by the gateway of the Christian Cemetery in Ramallah. He hadn't engraved just crosses, but angels with wings. His work was so perfect you could fancy the angels' wings were really moving when the wind blew.

I asked Abu Abdullah, the guard at the cemetery, about this artist. I knew, of course, what the answer would be: "Oh, he died years ago!" But, to my surprise, the guard said:

"He only died a few months back. If you'd come back a bit earlier, you might have seen him."

After a while he took me to see the grave of Daoud Ibrahim Rizkallah—not Rayan al-Taweel, as I'd called him. In my book I'd described the death of the creative artist Rayan al-Taweel. The real artist, Daoud Rizkallah, had died peacefully on March 13, 1996.

I took a walk through the cemetery, where his artistry still lived on. Angels bearing wreaths, angels kissing pictures, priests praying, others holding the cross. Some of his statues were still in good condition, others had tumbled to the ground. A broken marble angel whose heart was still beating, his spirit still haunting the place.

If only I'd asked about Daoud the first time I visited the cemetery! I might, perhaps, have been able to compare the artist in my text with the one who'd truly existed. I'd thought, at the time, how sad he would have been, because what the guard Abu Abdallah called the "Jews' computer" had invaded even the cemetery, with its printed pictures of the dead. Those pictures were as cold as death itself, and as dark as the marble stones beneath which the dead lay.

The body of Karim Khalaf was borne from his home on the hill, where the pine trees overlooked the blue sea, to his everlasting home at the cemetery, where pines spread their shade over the tombstone, to help give the grave some sense of warmth, to lessen the sense of loneliness and wipe away the dreadful face of death.

In 1926, when he donated an Ottoman Riyal to have the cemetery built, did Karim Khalaf's father or grandfather ever think that one day it would receive the body of Karim, who'd occupy its most beautiful grave?

On June 2, 1980, Ramallah was rocked by an explosion that rent the silence of the early summer morning, and ripped apart the car of the mayor, Karim Khalaf, as well as his leg, which later had to be amputated. The Israeli intelligence services had, at the same time, planted a similar device targeting the mayor of Nablus, Bassam al-Shakaa, who lost both his legs.

The echo of those two explosions reached the city of Beirut. That same day I hurried to see Naji al-Ali, to ask for his help in preparing a poster to mark the occasion. He naturally agreed, immediately fetching a piece of cardboard and sketching two men with legs like the trunks of trees, their roots sinking deep into the ground. Next morning the walls of Beirut were covered with copies of this poster.

Five years later, on March 30, 1985, the "Day of the Land," the earth received the body of Karim Khalaf. He'd been born in 1936, a year of special meaning in Palestinian history, marking as it did the start of the revolution and the great strike. He'd elected to leave us on the day the earth blossomed with flowers, sunshine, and joy.

I stood gazing at the grave, splendidly built, adorned with a verse from the Quran: "True men who never betrayed God. Some died and some are still waiting, but they never changed." There was another verse, from the Gospel: "I am the way, the truth, and the life"; and "God has his angels guard your steps." There were also two lines of poetry from different poems, one speaking of the homeland, the other of the strong will of the people that can break any chain.

Two lions of black marble guarded the grave, and a picture of the dead man who had left us, yet was able, still, to roam the streets, making sure the town and its people were safe and sound, before returning, at the day's end, to lie in peace beneath the marble tombstone.

~ 10 ~

The verses adorning Karim Khalaf's stone told the story of two towns that had begun centuries before and had helped unite Muslims and Christians, tearing down the barriers between them, so they could live in peace and tranquility, free from all recrimination and doctrinal quarrel.

Ramallah, like every town, had its own story, a story the citizens would tell their young children in the dark and dreary winter nights. And, like all the stories people liked to tell, that of the town of Ramallah had been embellished, to add a magical touch and blur the lines between fact and fancy. Each would tell his own version, and the beauty that emerged was better than any painstaking search for the facts.

The Crusaders, who invaded the land blessed by the footsteps of all the prophets and saints, had (according to Rey, the French historian) come to a place called Ramelie—which was, I presume, none other than Ramallah. The Crusaders stayed in the place for almost a hundred years, leaving behind an olive oil press that remained in use until the start of the twentieth century.

With the Crusaders' departure, Ramallah became a deserted village, full of trees and empty homes, till at last, at the end of the sixteenth century, Rashed al-Haddadin and his people came there from the eastern part of Jordan, fleeing the injustice of a sultan who threatened their safety and honor.

It's told how the tyrant prince of the Karak-Shawbak region, whose name was Diyab Ibn Qaisoum, had been the guest of Rashed bin Saqr al-Haddad, the chief of a Christian clan that enjoyed cordial relations with the Muslim Banaweyeh clan. The two had made a pact to come to one another's aid in time of need.

While the prince was sitting with his host at al-Haddadin guest house, news arrived to Rashed al-Haddad that he was now the father of a baby girl; this child, later named Hind, would one day be the cause of the town of Ramallah's founding, following the heedless words spoken by her father.

"What's my share of the good news?,"[11] the prince asked his host.

Without thinking, Rashed al-Haddad at once replied: "The girl is yours!"

He little knew the bitter price he would have to pay for uttering those words—words that would later cost him his homeland. Whether he was simply being courteous, or, indeed, merely joking, he must have known the difference of religion would mean the promise could never be fulfilled.

It seems, though, that the prince was prepared to accept no excuses, or to make any allowance for jokes or passing remarks.

He also had a most sharp and long memory.

When Hind was of age, Prince Ibn Qaisoum sent his convoy to the Haddadin tribe to ask for the daughter's hand in marriage for his son, in fulfillment of the promise made twelve years before. But the delegation returned empty-handed to the prince, who had taken no account of the difference in religion and was furious at the rejection. Ibn Qaisoum accordingly threatened the tribe, which decided to be true to its beliefs, though knowing full well it would have, sooner or later, to pay for the stance it had adopted. The prince had two young men from the tribe kidnapped, then asked for the bride to be sent as a ransom for their release.

In the face of this challenge, the Haddadin tribe decided to sacrifice the lives of the two young men, who were brutally killed: the prince ordered they should be bound to heavy rocks and rolled over a tall cliff. From that day on, the name of the place, formerly Batin al-Taweel, became Madhal Awlad al-Haddad (the place from which the children of al-Haddad were rolled).

After this tragic event, Rashed al-Haddad realized, belatedly, how weak his position was, and that any confrontation with Ibn Qaisoum would end badly for him. So, he decided to leave and save his family from further danger. The only one to whom he could turn for help was his friend Hussein, from the neighboring Muslim Banaweyeh tribe. Hussein too had suffered from Ibn Qaisoum's injustice, and he felt bound to support his Christian friend. They decided to leave and head west, beyond the Dead Sea.

Imagination played its part in the beautiful portrayal of Christian–Muslim unity. According to the traditional tales, Rashed al-Haddad led Ibn Qaisoum's men to believe he'd agreed to his daughter's marriage to the young prince, and invited them to come. A fierce battle then took place, and Ibn Qaisoum's men, including the prospective bridegroom, were slaughtered. The story was a living reminder of the famous Kala'a massacre, which put an end to the Mamluk Dynasty in Egypt.

The tale would reach its climax with a picture of Ibn Qaisoum's army pursuing the two tribes as they fled toward the Dead Sea. There, at the shallow part of the Dead Sea, Rashed and Hussein planted sickles, swords, spears and sharp pieces of iron well prepared by Rashed, the blacksmith. Ibn Qaisoum's horses, rushing into the salty water, were caught by these sharp instruments. They bled so much that the water became red with their blood. At last the men of Ibn Qaisoum were overcome, and retreated covered in blood, water, and salt.

The two friends managed to get to safety at the other side of the River Jordan. They reached Halhoul, near al-Khalil (Hebron), then moved on to Bethlehem, and there it was that they first heard of an abandoned place to the north of Jerusalem with large numbers of trees, known as Ramallah. They at once decided to go there, and the trees in Ramallah provided the blacksmith, Rashed al-Haddad, with all the wood he needed to make fire for his work.

One of the delightful things said about the place was that the thick oak trees on the Majnouna Road, with their tangled branches, stopped even the cats from roaming the place, as well anything swooping down from the sky.

Al-Bireh, though, was inhabited at the time, and apparently the tribe living there, the Gazawneh, sold the land of Ramallah to Rashed. Hussein, for his part, elected to live in al-Bireh among its Muslim citizens. All the families of al-Bireh, so it was said, were descended from the tribe of Hussein, with no information on any trace left of the Gazawneh tribe.

~ 11 ~

*A*in al-Bireh, Ain al-Bourj, Ain al-Balad, Ain Sama'an, Ain al-Jawz, Ain Mizrab, Ain Munjed, Ain Um al-Kurzum, Ain Misbaah, Ain Um al-Sharayet—these and numerous other springs were for many years scattered through the small mountainous region where homes for the two towns were built, and united by a sip of water.

Al-Bireh derived its name from the Ain al-Bireh spring. The word *bi-irawt* meant "well" in the Canaanite language, while *birta* meant "fortress" in Aramaic.

I went off to try and find what might remain of these springs, and, after a lengthy search, found Ain Misbaah among homes that were unfamiliar, quite different from what I'd stored up in my memory.

The place around the springs had once been vacant and tranquil, the silence broken only by the sound of the cicadas. The Ain Misbaah spring was running below an old stone arch, which was more than two times taller than my height. Women who used to fill their jars with the spring's water moved freely inside the arch. Today, however, it has astonishingly shrunk into a tiny trickle of water. Was the spring almost exhausted, or was I so old now, so utterly senile, that I'd started mixing up the visions of former times?

Despite the many springs in the two towns, the simple word "al-Ain" would always mean Ain al-Bireh, next to which a mosque had been built, known as the al-Ain Mosque, and, from the early sixties on, there'd been a park alongside it, called al-Bireh Park.

The park was still being laid out when my family moved into one of the modern buildings being erected opposite. That was when the wealth coming in from the Gulf was just beginning to be felt in my family, when my brothers went to work in Kuwait one after the other and started financially to support our father, just as every son did at that bygone time.

Moving into one of those new buildings put up by expatriates of al-Bireh and Ramallah working and living in America, was viewed then as a token of change in social status. The buildings had stairs insects and mice couldn't get up, and they had toilets and bathrooms with coal-heated water. Every home had an electric bell that let out a soft ring when pressed, giving those living there a delightful sense of belonging to high society.

I stood beneath the balcony where I'd slept one summer night. I was still just a teenager when a woman crawled into my cold bed, to become the first woman ever to keep me warm, with whom I experienced my first teenage fantasies. The woman who visited my humble dreams was none other than Jacqueline Kennedy!

I now passed under the balcony of what had once been my home—a home that, for all its warmth, had lacked for me the warmth of living in a quarter. But the building embodied a new social status, although the people who lived there were mostly peasants who still kept up their old traditions of leaving the doors of their apartments open for the neighbors. One had only to say "Dastour,"[12] and take two steps inside, to become one of the family.

In the apartment opposite, I'd made friends with two brothers: Issam, a year older than I was, and Hisham, who was a year younger.

I used to compete with Issam in procuring oil paints and imitating and copying the drawings of Ismail Shamout.[13] Issam was better than me in securing the paints, but I was better in drawing. I even won the school drawing competition one year, producing a portrait of President Nasser in charcoal (even though it was forbidden then to have pictures of the late president). Hisham, the younger brother, used to challenge me to poetry recitals, and always won.

Hisham was, so everyone believed, destined to become a famous poet, on account of his ability to memorize poetry. He had only to hear one of his brothers recite a poem and he could repeat it word for word. One day he embarrassed his older brother, Aref, by memorizing a poem no one in Aref's class had been able to learn. No one ever knew how Aref's teacher had come to hear of Hisham's feat—a feat beyond students three years older than he was. He called Hisham up, had him recite the poem, then told his lazy students to line up, so that each could get a slap in the face from Hisham, the prospective poet.

This same Hisham, who is in his fifties now and might, by this time, have forgotten everything to do with poetry, is the same man who stands up in front of thousands of Germans gathered to hear him speak, addressing them in their own language as a leader of the Green Party and its representative to the German parliament.

Very close to that building were the lost footsteps of a small child who no one had known would, one day, become the master of the universe.

There, where al-Ain spring and al-Ain Mosque were located, women used to come with their jars and crowd around the spring that had enough water for all. By the side of the road descending to al-Shurfa Quarter, parallel to the Jerusalem road, there was a long pool where animals came to drink. The water would flow to reach the land by the foot of al-Taweel mountain, watering the fig and quince trees. For many years, in spring the mountainside was covered with wild thyme, and would welcome the birds, which were good for hunting. Young children, of whom I was one, would go and race among the wild flowers growing on the slope and around the rocks.

In the mid-sixties, there was a rumor—because of the war, it couldn't be verified—that al-Taweel mountain was about to be sold to some Arab businessmen from the Gulf, who were convinced the town was a tourist attraction. The widely read Kuwaiti magazine *Al-Arabi* had devoted its cover and twenty pages to this lovely place, with colored illustrations, recommending it specifically to anyone in search of the best fresh air in the world. For all the expectations and promises of prosperity, people were skeptical about the project and viewed it with distress.

So, you can imagine my own distress when someone I knew told me, pointing at the same time to the slope of al-Taweel Mountain, that the spring's water had become polluted. And imagine, too, the pain and heartache I felt when I looked up and saw a Jewish settlement had been built on the summit of the mountain, crushing, together, my memories, and the flowers, and all the quince trees that would never grow again.

The settlement was called Psagot, and I didn't even bother to search out the meaning of the name. I didn't want to rid myself of the pain and distress coursing through my heart and blood. I wanted my memory to remain vigilant, able to free al-Taweel Mountain from the concrete claws of the Jewish Psagot.

It was there, close by the spring with its polluted water, that we lost al-Taweel Mountain. And it was there, where I was standing now, that, twenty centuries before, a small child had become lost from his mother. His name was Jesus!

According to the ancient story, Our Lady, Mary, and her little son were on their way from Nazareth to Bethlehem. They passed by al-Bireh, or Bi'rout as it then was called, and they lodged at a tiny inn near the spring. (Not the inn whose ruins still stood there, but an inn that was later turned into the Church of the Holy Family, which remained there till it was recently demolished. Some of its old stones could still be seen.)

When the mother went looking for her missing son, who was to be ever present in the human and spiritual history of mankind, she found him playing with children eager to welcome their beautiful guest. He hadn't heard his mother's footsteps as she searched for him, in great panic, in the streets and alleys of al-Bireh, unaware his small lost footsteps would bless the place forever.

As for the young lads of Bi'rout, could they ever have

dreamed, as they played with the small boy by the spring, splashing him with its water, that in just a few years he'd become the Messiah?

And could we ever have dreamt, when we were children waiting for our mothers to fill their jars with water near al-Taweel Mountain, which stood watching over them in their embroidered gowns and with the water trickling down through their breasts—could we ever have dreamed that the name of the mountain would vanish from our maps forever, to be replaced by Psagot?

～ 12 ～

The people who settled on al-Taweel Mountain, who built Psagot on the peak of Bi'rout, both changed and tarnished the geography of the place, falsifying history with their flawed mythology.

Invaders don't read history. What point would there be, after all, in reading anything that ran counter to their desire to invade, to expand and settle?

Yet history will always have the last word. Psagot, like any other settlement, embodies a double violation: of history and geography. And that's even before we begin to speak of politics, human rights, and international law.

Emigrants to the States from al-Bireh have told how in a corner of this vast world, they have found a map dating back to 3500BC on which Bi'rout appeared; as indeed it did in numerous chapters of the Bible, long before any mention of the city of Jerusalem.

Nor was Jesus, as a child, the only one to have walked in this place. Aaron's steps, so it's been said, were heard there, just as my own have been, and those of the settlers.

The Muslim Caliph Umar Ibn al-Khattab[14] also set his foot in al-Bireh, when he came to the Holy Land to receive the key to the city of Jerusalem. In accordance with his usual custom, the righteous caliph declined to pray in the Church of the Holy Family, as he had earlier declined to do in the Church of the Resurrection in Jerusalem. Instead the Mosque of Omar was built next to the church, being later destroyed, then rebuilt anew.

Salahuddin al-Ayyoubi [Saladin], who liberated the Holy Land, also passed through al-Bireh, and left his mark on the place.

Until recently, those invaders coming to al-Bireh from America, Europe, and the former Soviet Union would follow a yellow line, marked out on the asphalt to lead them to Psagot and prevent them, strangers that they were, from getting lost. This line passed close by al-Ain spring, al-Ain Mosque, and the Church of the Holy Family. During the years of the Intifada, falling snow would spread fear in the settlers' hearts whenever it covered the yellow line. For its disappearance meant losing their way to the settlement, and so straying into the old town of al-Bireh, where the young men were little disposed to welcome a wandering Jew of this kind!

Although al-Bireh was the more ancient, the name Ramallah came to represent al-Bireh and Ramallah combined. As one who never owned any land in either town, I never quite knew where I stood, or why I'd say Ramallah when I really meant al-Bireh.

According to my birth certificate, I was born in al-Bireh. Yet my green identity card, issued by the Palestinian Authority with a lavish use of Hebrew characters, said I was born in Ramallah. I raised no objection, never questioning the matter. The truth was that—as I liked to answer when asked where I was born—I was happy to be a son of the two towns of Ramallah and al-Bireh.

Ramallah, the closest place on earth to the Canaanite House of God, originally meant "mountain" ("height" in the ancient Aramaic language), to which the Arabs then added the name of the Almighty. Open though the town always was to modernity, it remained proud of its ancient roots, especially when some old pieces of pottery were found in the Tira district, once known as Kafr Ghamla. The remains of Saint Stephen, the first Christian martyr, were discovered in Ramallah.

In the old caves near Ain Misbah, so it's said, was found a lead casket dating back to the third century AD, bearing various engraved symbols, some pagan, some Christian.

Up to the middle of the twentieth century, the ancient town of Ramallah cradled the church of Abraham. This was later transformed into a mosque, then into a shrine that eventually fell into ruin in 1957,[15] along with so many other places destined to ruin in that ill-fated year.

The place of those without place, the refuge for those without refuge!

It was actually possible to be standing on one side of the road in al-Bireh and talking to a friend who was on the opposite side in Ramallah. The Lighthouse Square, though, was divided equally between the two towns.

The blending of the two towns was all the odder in that Ramallah belonged to the Christians and al-Bireh to the Muslims. This created a novel multi-religious phenomenon, and an integrated relationship between the two towns, which might have led to total merger but for a persistence in keeping the two towns ultimately separate through having an independent municipality for each town. The place kept growing, and it benefited from this constant rivalry.

Ramallah/al-Bireh was, then, a twin nurtured by emulation and healthy rivalry. In the early sixties, al-Bireh laid out a beautiful park, which attracted the children of both towns with its brightly colored swings, while the adults, coming from all Palestinian towns, enjoyed their family gatherings there. Not too long after, Ramallah initiated its own park project, and invited the young people to perform folk dances to songs especially written by Hadiyya Abdul-Hadi for the summer festival hosted by the town; al-Bireh, then, invited the same writer to produce a play for their own festival, and even went one step further by inviting the Lebanese singer Taroub to perform in the park. I still remembered how all the family and neighbors gathered on the roof of the Shukri Shaker building where we lived, to watch this famous singer, who'd come all the way from Lebanon. When Ramallah's public library began attracting the educated people of the two towns, as well as pupils whose teachers had managed to convince them of the benefits of reading, al-Bireh founded a public library of its own. Inspecting my two membership cards to the two libraries, which I still had thirty years on, I found they looked just the same apart from the name of the town and the color. If a road was opened in one town, then two would be opened in the other. Let a school be built in one town, and you'd be sure to find two spring up in the other. One person would emigrate to the US from one of the two towns, and ten persons would inevitably emigrate from the other. Even the young women of the two towns would dream of the same Prince Charming: invariably some lawyer, doctor, or engineer, with an American citizenship, who spoke broken Arabic!

One question I pondered constantly: What was the secret of this place, the thing that balanced all these attracting and repelling forces? Why did the people of the two towns leave, and what attracted outsiders to come in?

It was the magic of the virgin site, perhaps, that attracted Rashed al-Haddad and his friend Hussein. Later Ramallah saw the flow of Christian immigrants, to be followed still later by Muslims. What increased the social variety of the two towns was the great wave of refugees from all the various Palestinian towns and villages, including Jaffa, Lydd, and Ramleh, in the wake of the Jewish occupation in 1948.

The forests of Ramallah held the memories of those fleeing wretched refugees, who found shelter in the shade of the tall trees, and received the help they needed from its people. These images were later portrayed by Aref al-Aref[16] in his work on *al-Nakba* [the Palestinian catastrophe]. (He may have written it in that beautiful house with the tiled roof, which was later converted into "Gallery 79"—its frontage eventually blocked out by one of those modern buildings!).

Ramallah attracted the vegetable merchants from Lydd, along with the smart merchants from al-Khalil [Hebron]. And before 1967 Ramallah emerged as the center of the Palestinian intelligentsia, who provided Jerusalem with the articles for its newspapers. After the occupation it became the major center for cultural activities, with numbers of writers, dramatists, and artists coming there to live from various towns. And now it's been able, once more, to attract some of those coming back home. It's been suggested indeed that Ramallah should be declared the cultural, economic, and administrative capital of the nascent Palestinian State.

With all these forces of attraction, those of repulsion remain difficult to understand.

Ramallah, it's remarkable to note, is no longer inhabited by its indigenous people, the great-grandchildren of Rashed al-Haddad. This has given rise to numerous questions of a sociological nature. Could it be that the people of Ramallah were entranced by the magical winds of America? Perhaps.

Yussef Awdeh al-Debbini (whose name shows him to have come originally from the forests of Debbin in the Ajloun Heights in North Jordan) was the first pioneer to answer the enticement of the American dream after the tempting tales that spurred people to leave for that vast and prosperous land. In 1895, Ramallah's Columbus went off to the New World, to be followed three years later by another early pioneer, Issa Ishaq, who astonished the town with the money he'd transfer back to his father.

It was homesickness that lay behind the making of al-Mughtaribreen Square in Ramallah, and the building of the al-Mughtaribreen School in al-Bireh, next to the church and the mosque of the same name. But, for all that, longing for Ramallah wasn't enough to fill the demographic gap that emerged with regard to the descendants of Rashed al-Haddad and his friend Hussein, the indigenous people of the twin towns. Their numbers declined, while ever more people flooded in from the Palestinian villages and towns occupied by Jews in 1948 and also from those that were not occupied. It was in the light of this that in the early eighties Khalil Abu Daya, a native of Ramallah, wrote in his book that 85 percent of native Ramallah people lived in the US. And, in the same decade, Abdul Aziz Shaheen published a book on the families of Ramallah. The number of Ramallah emigrants now living in the US was 10,000, while the entire population of Ramallah didn't exceed 15,000!

~ 13 ~

*I*n the early sixties both towns spoke highly of a woman who'd taken up the challenge and gotten an education, going into the examination hall with one of her children to get her high-school certificate. Nearly thirty years later she opted for another challenge: this time she wanted to run for the presidency, as the sole candidate against Yasser Arafat!

Samiha Khalil—or Aunt Um Khalil, as everyone in al-Bireh called her—was a woman carved from stone, and born for challenge. She worked like a silkworm, was untiringly busy as a bee. She took her love of life from the trees: as branches cast their shade, so she spread her love to all those in need of tenderness.

In 1965 she rented a small house near the Friends' School and announced she was founding an association for the revival of the family [Society of In'ash el-Usra]. Um Khalil was a dreamer, people said. But a dream nurtured by so much hard work was bound to become reality.

I visited the association, which in due course became a large institute and lived on at the national museum. The place reflected a glory long past, but it did its level best to defy a project that works on thrusting our people, our history, our civilization, and our creativity into the corners of oblivion.

Leaving the association, I went in search of a place that meant a great deal to me—surely it had been somewhere around here. My elementary school.

A woman walked out of what had once been the third elementary class and asked me if I was looking for something. I shook my head, though actually I was looking for everything.

After leaving Mrs. Adla's preschool, I went—or rather it was decided I should go—to the school set up in the very house the woman had just exited, on the left side of the street leading to al-Balou, on the Nablus road. The parents of the students, and the people of al-Bireh generally, hadn't taken to the name Ubada Ibn as-Samit—the Companion of the Prophet after whom the school had been named—and had decided to call the school after the family that owned the house. It was known, accordingly, as the Mutawi School. Ubada Ibn as-Samit remained just an unfamiliar name written on the black sign.

I've recalled my school throughout my life, above all whenever I've smelled anything akin to sheep's wool and dung. I remember, too, how little I enjoyed the start of the school year. I was always a week or two late starting, even a couple of months sometimes, because I'd be going to orthopedists in Amman and Jericho and Jerusalem, or to the lovely old hospital in Ramallah, which was pulled down just days before my return. I was standing there now and gazing at the rubble, remembering my past painful experience.

I was overjoyed when, one day, I went back to my classroom and saw my real name written in the school records. I'd had to use the false name Yunis to have an operation paid for by the UNRWA. This was one of the tricks devised by the fertile Palestinian mind when the welfare association, for one reason or another, mistreated someone or seized his identity card.

If I was never top student, this wasn't just because I was always late for the school year. The fact is, a student called Nizar always came first, passing with honors. This clever boy was from al-Bireh, and he was very loyal to his father, a Communist who'd been arrested and imprisoned in al-Jafr desert prison. Everyone respected his tireless desire to be always top of the class. Abandoning all hope of this myself, I tried to make up by filling the four walls of the classroom with posters I'd written out in my beautiful handwriting. All the lazy teachers would have me copy their own papers for them, and ever since then I've loathed copying out any document.

One of the many images and memories springing out from the place was that tense moment when our principal, Yaqoub Hasan (Abu Jamal) told us:

"Go off now, all of you—one at a time—leave the school and go home, now. Run—run straight home, don't stop for a second, whatever you see on the way. Or else!"

He was gritting his teeth, as he always did. He didn't have time to explain what the "or else" meant. The young devils racing through the streets melted in the crowds gathered near the huge mulberry tree that shaded the Hasan al-Aaraj Café, opposite the old municipal building. And there the children added their voices to the crowds demonstrating and yelling:

"Down with Glubb! Down with Glubb!" The slogan was as simple and clear, as it could be, in meaning and sound alike, and the children went on repeating it for years on end, even after General Glubb had left the scene![17]

I stood in front of what had once been a café. The round iron tables and wooden chairs had been consigned to oblivion, and the whole place was now a paved square where more profitable goods of various kinds were sold.

I recalled the waiter who served at the tables there, a hunchback who'd spent his whole life waiting on people as they drank coffee, played cards and backgammon, and smoked a *nargila*.[18] He carried a metal tray, along with the burden of his hunched back the size of a football, while moving among the tables nestled there beneath the shade of a mulberry tree. The tree's delicious fruit lay crushed beneath the customers' feet, while the waiter smelling of coffee and burnt sugar moved among them.

The hunchback was gone now, and so was the voice of Abd al-Nasser, who could once be heard from the radio resting on a wooden shelf in one of the corners of the café. Leaning forward to hear the radio was something new and unfamiliar in those days.

I gazed at the mulberry tree, its shade smaller now, like its branches and leaves. There it stood, looking frail and naked, waiting for some fool to saw it down, or some crazed, ingenious artist to turn it to a piece of art revealing the secrets of life.

~ 14 ~

*I*n time I had to grow up, and so did my classmates, and the Mutawi School grew narrower than the dreams and slogans that filled our roving imaginations.

One school year, on the first day, we were put in line and taken to a new school set up on the Jerusalem road. The al-Bireh New School certainly was new then! Its gate was on the street leading to Jerusalem; then, for a reason and at a time I had never known, it was moved to a side lane.

It was there, in this building on the edge of al-Amaari Camp, that I learned for the first time what a proper school looked like: the long corridors, the wide staircase, and the lines of arches. It was a different world from the place, basically just a rented house, where I'd just spent my five elementary years.

The director of the al-Bireh New School was Mr. Rifaat al-Shihabi, who was able to hide all keys to his personality and so remained an unknown, vague person to us all. His looks were like the crack of a whip. He had only to glance at us and all thought of movement would vanish. Our hearts would pound as we stood there, trembling like wild trees swaying this way and that in a winter storm. Then Mr. Shihabi would pick out a student he'd decided might be tempted to misbehave and would slap him on the face, so hard I can hear the echo now.

It was at that school, even so, that I first discovered the literary bent that would pave the way for the vice known as writing, with all its limitless pleasures.

One day, on the spur of an emotional, patriotic moment, our Arabic teacher, Naim Attieh, called on all his students to write an essay titled "Standing Behind the Wire." It was then that I knew, for the first time, the delight that writing could arouse.

I wrote. I wrote as if I'd been standing behind that wire for thousands of years. I felt the pain and agony my sad heart had known deep down for many years. I harnessed my fingers to the skill of writing, and to words telling the story of the sad sun and its golden rays setting beyond the imprisoned horizon. I wrote of the bleeding sea sick for home, the weary, paralyzed armies, the days awaiting the feasts. On that day a new horizon opened and from then on I was involved in writing.

If I had to, I could find that whole text, safe and sound in my memory. Mr. Naim Attieh had me go into every class at the al-Bireh New School and read my essay, and by the end I had it almost by heart.

I had great hopes for my friend Waddah, who shared my school desk and had the creative talent to go along with my madcap ideas. I suggested we might prepare an issue of a magazine with both text and illustrations. Then we could circulate it among the students for a piaster a night, and raise enough money to allow us to bring out a second issue or even print the magazine.

So, we bought a big notebook with a hard cover, along with some watercolors and Chinese ink, and started writing articles and stories and producing illustrations. The first issue of *Al-Jeel al-Saeed* [The New Generation] duly emerged, and finally, three years later, we were able to mimeograph the magazine. A lifelong friendship was born between Waddah and myself, and is still alive now—though Waddah contrived to divert all that foolishness into architecture, which took him away from writing and drawing.

It was at that school that I laid the foundation for another close friendship, with Talaat, who later joined the magazine's editorial committee. Talaat was the son of the *mukhtar*, or mayor, of al-Amaari [refugee] Camp. He enjoyed talking politics—though his disgusting stories about what took place in the fragrant garden of the camp, in the toilets of the camp's school, were more interesting than any views he held on Arnold Toynbee or Dale Carnegie!

~ 15 ~

The Friends' School always stayed out of reach, even though it was very near my home. People of my class simply didn't belong in the place, so any dream of going there was likely to stay a dream. One of the chief things I missed out on was never learning to speak English with a proper accent—not like all those lucky, pampered students that boys like me were so jealous of. We'd get back at them by saying they were more like girls! The Friends' School, however, with its old premises and its greenery, stayed fresh in my memory, and in the history of Ramallah/al-Bireh.

The town had always abandoned its rural seclusion when a Christian mission came to set up an institute, welcoming its initiatives to open up the world to us. In 1869, when Ramallah wasn't regarded as even a potential town, two members of the Friends, a man and his wife, came with plans for opening a girls' school. The young girls of the time (the great-grandmothers of today's young girls—we're talking, remember, about a project a hundred and thirty years ago, in Ottoman times) greeted this with heartfelt enthusiasm. At the beginning of the twentieth century, as recorded on its stones, the Friends' School for Boys was set up.

Through all the hard times the town had seen, the old Victorian premises still stood there in all their dignity, and none of the theater halls in other schools, or in the town generally, could begin to rival the Khalil Tawtah Hall at the Friends' School.

Some men were working to renovate the theater. It appeared smaller than the building I'd kept stored in the memory I was now striving to refresh. I recalled the first time I entered it, and how in awe I was of what I saw. My family hadn't managed to get me to bed, and so I went with them to watch my brother Ali play the part of a miser in what may have been one of Molière's plays. I clapped long and hard for my brother, whose acting was as good as his goalkeeping. Before leaving for Kuwait, he left me his treasure: some old brushes and oil paints. He could never have dreamed how, by doing this, he'd paved the way for me to stand, a few years later, on that very same stage, to receive the top award for two portraits, one titled *President Nasser* and another, *Dead without Graves* [*Morts sans sépulture*], the title of a play I'd read by Jean-Paul Sartre. This was during the festival of the Parade of Art, a cultural event set up and patronized by the educator Amin Hafez al-Dajani, one that became a Ramallah tradition, celebrated each year.

I stood on the sidewalk opposite the School for the Blind and gazed at the great Friends' School stadium, recalling its evergreen grass and the tall eucalyptus trees all around it. This, of course, was in the days before artificial grass was discovered.

It grieved me to see the damage and signs of neglect so evident in this stadium where we'd once played. The attendants had never been able to prevent us from playing there, even though, unable to use its full length, we could only run the width of it.

There was a very solid reason why I insisted on transferring from al-Bireh New School to Ramallah Preparatory School, even though the latter was set up in an old brick house on the outskirts of old Ramallah, and didn't even look like a proper school. At that time my family had moved into a house in al-Masayef Street, near al-Mughtaribreen Square and the Cinema al-Jamil, and, standing on the southern balcony, I could hear the voice of Jamila Bouhaired, as Rushdi Abaza tortured her with an electric rod.

But there was a hidden reason, more important than all the obvious ones. There was a time when, as I walked down the main street each morning on my way to school, I'd gaze into the eyes of my first love, and feel the magical quiver and pounding heart that brightened my whole day. It's a feeling I've never been able to describe.

The move to the new school became urgent one evening when my sister Muyassar (before she went to join my brothers in Kuwait, leaving the house plunged in silence) came back home with a verbal message and flowers from my sweetheart!

Further reasons were the extra day off on Sunday and the reputation of the school's principal, Ahmad Thalji, who was known to be very tolerant compared with Rifaat al-Shihabi at al-Bireh New School, at whose hands we suffered such terrors.

The building (which now looks fit for anything but a

school) gave me a sense of coziness and intimacy. There were no playgrounds, and this gave us an excuse to slip out into the streets behind the school to buy sandwiches and sweets, and to watch the girl students of the Friends' School without being punished or reprimanded.

When the Arabic teacher at this new school, Mr. Zaidan Abu Zayyad, found among my books Ahmad Rami's translation of al-Khayyam's poems, I thought he was going to reprimand me. But, to my surprise, he asked me to recite some of the poems at the school's open day. I remember how proud I felt, standing there, reciting in front of my father, friends, principal and teachers:

What waste to live a day without love!

Mr. Zaidan knew well enough how to utilize my artistic and cultural gifts, encouraging me to issue a news bulletin to rival the only other bulletin, issued by second preparatory class B.

When the bulletin was released, the students gathered to read it, wide-eyed. Just one student came up to shake my hand and congratulate me. My bulletin, he told me politely, was better than the one he brought out. He was also the only student at the school who wore glasses!

Next day, Yasser and I found ourselves chasing after a beautiful girl tourist, on the pretext that we wanted to explain to her about the Palestinian cause. There were just two major problems: we lacked a detailed understanding of the cause, and we couldn't discuss the matter properly in English!

The two of us were to go a long way in life. When *Al-Jeel al-Saeed* [The New Generation] magazine was mimeographed two years later, Yasser joined the editorial committee and, simultaneously, we combined to issue the news bulletin. We made it our goal that the bulletin should find its way to the Girls' School, and we also made sure the girls won most of the bulletin's competitions, even if it meant passing them the correct answers. From that time on, our paths were destined to cross daily.

Rizk was another who'd cleverly exploit my creative skills. He was the friend and classmate with whom I shared a desk filled with engraved hearts struck by Cupid. He was always full of vitality and life, and this made him the most mischievous student in the whole school—no one bothered to try and compete with him. One day he came up to me, heartbroken, because his sweetheart insisted on ignoring him totally. He drove me into a corner by saying:

"You're the only one who can help!"

He went on to explain.

"You have such beautiful handwriting, and you know how to write to make her heart ache. Then there's your friend Nizar Qabbani—you know all his poems by heart, he could be a big help.[19] Write me a letter, and I'll give it to her. You can pull it off, I'm sure you can!"

So, I wrote a letter to Hanan, from the depths of my friend's heart. What use were my writing skills, after all, if I couldn't help a friend in need, and in love?

To our joint amazement, Hanan replied very swiftly, pouring out her love and passion for the dark young man who was so madly in love with her. We were surprised, too, to see that after just a few years at the Friends' School (she'd spent her early years in America, where she was born), she had beautiful

Arabic handwriting, while her language sounded as fresh and lively as though it were coming from rose gardens and the wings of butterflies.

I had to go on writing. I couldn't back out now, and let Rizk's poor language and sprawling handwriting spoil an impossible love formed by my own hands. My warm, loving words had carried out their first mission on earth.

Things would have developed differently had I not happened, at a friend's house, to meet with Hind, a very beautiful girl who wore revealing clothes and had a bubbly character. She was fit to win a Friends' School beauty contest. In those days the basic rule for getting acquainted was to exchange autographs, and that's what we did, writing friendly words in our colored autograph notebooks. When we returned the notebooks, we got a shock: not from the words themselves, but from the style, and also from the handwriting.

There in front of Hind were Rizk's words to Hanan, and in front of me were Hanan's words to Rizk. We read the questions in one another's eyes—and also the love story of two of our friends, doomed to failure now.

Our eyes met and silently discussed the matter. Neither said a word, and we never met again. All we knew, after that remarkable meeting, was that Rizk and Hanan never exchanged a love letter again.

~ 16 ~

Opposite the rubble of what had once been a two-story brick-roofed hospital stood a place that stirred memories of events, teachers, students, and friends.

The premises of Ramallah High School looked much smaller and much older. It was as though the ashes of the old days lay there in the dark corners of the rooms. Yet, for all that, it stood firm, holding on to the old times—my times.

I went to Ramallah High School at an age when all the fantasies were blossoming together: fantasies of knowledge and creativity, of women, of falling in love and being loved.

The mid-sixties brought changes to our plans, in politics and culture alike. We were a group of friends, taking pride in what we'd accomplished—bringing out a magazine that would sell 300 issues. Later we embarked on a further project, to set up a league for young writers and artists, but the war confined this to some papers I still have with me, along with copies of the two issues of the magazine that did emerge.

Our respective choices, of scientific and literary studies, meant that we went to different schools: Waddah and Talaat to the Hashemite School, Yasser and I to Ramallah High School. Splitting up like this helped enrich our educational experience. Waddah and Talaat, at the Hashemite School, met a left-leaning Arabic teacher who wrote stories calling for solidarity with the poor. And at Ramallah High School the two of us met his counterpart, another leftist and one of the most prominent critics at *Al-Ufuq al-Jadeed* [The New Horizon] magazine brought out by a poet from al-Bireh called Amin Shunnar.

The Arabic teacher at the Hashemite School was Mahmoud Shukair, and his counterpart at Ramallah High School was Khalil al-Sawahiri. The two men came from the same village, and because of this they were constantly together, quite apart from their similar political views and choices of career, and their roles as pillars of *The New Horizon*. They helped bridge the gap between the two schools in Ramallah.

My first article, published in the Jerusalem newspaper *Al-Jihad* at the end of 1965, was entitled, "Modern Art has a Message," and expressed a staunch support for modernity in the fine arts, even though all my own paintings, exhibited at the Ramallah School for Girls in 1964, belonged to the classical school. The article seems to have reflected a major change I was undergoing, influenced especially by Freud's theory of psychoanalysis, which I used in my argument on the message of modern art, and which formed the basis for a radical change from the classical art, with all its limitations, to the vast and colorful freedom of modernity in art, which knew no boundaries. The change led me to a totally different path, as I turned from painting to writing.

My teacher, Mr. Khalil al-Sawahiri, had read my article even before I had the chance to know it had been published. He praised it in front of all my classmates, then asked me if I'd written anything else. I gave him the text of a story I'd written, entitled *Al-Urjooha* [The Swing]. He was impressed, and, to my surprise, had it published in the *Filasteen* newspaper along with a critical account he'd written on it. It was the first criticism I'd had.

Perhaps it was Freud, and later Dostoyevsky, with his skill in penetrating to the inner soul, who led me to choose psychology as my major at university. Whatever the reason, that first published article of mine definitely introduced me to the fever, and pleasure and vice of writing.

Amid the flow of articles, I effortlessly forgot all about fine art, which had been the subject of my first article. It was a quarter of a century, after a very long slumber, before my love of painting awoke once more.

As I looked from the window of Mahmoud Shuqayr's room at the Ministry of Culture in Ramallah, it pleased me that I could see the place where I had been born. I was also pleased to recapture those old days, filled with rich dreams and spiritual quest for inner self discovery amid the confusion of books and words.

Undoubtedly the fact that Mr. Shuqayr was responsible for part of the back page in the daily *Al-Jihad* helped build a creative platform for a whole generation trying out its first steps in the world of writing. Three decades ago he wrote an article on that generation, in which he discussed stories by such rising writers as Walid Saif, Samir Is-haq, Mahmoud al-Rimawi, Farouq Wadi, and Laila al-Atrash. He also pinpointed distinctive works by Fuad Abu Hijla, Raja Fuad Raja, Mahmoud Shaker al-Khateeb, Yussef Abdulaziz, Mahmoud Ibrahim al-Ghoubaish, and Azmi al-Shu'aibi. Some of these are still involved in the world of writing, while others have taken a totally different course.

Mahmoud Shuqayr changed his ironic style after the defeat of June 1967, never returning to the satire for which he'd been so noted. He may even have forgotten that he once wrote a column called "Cultural Gossip," with "The Chatterbox" as his pseudonym. I was pleased when, one day, he devoted his column to the plans for setting up a "Cultural League," in which I was involved. The project never materialized, though, because of the war.

The educational theories of the time didn't concern themselves with the teacher–student relationship. But many of the teachers at Ramallah High School had, in practice, already built up a democratically based relation with their students. They had no need to dig it out of educational textbooks.

Memory took me back to Mr. Ahmad Fahim Jabr, who taught me philosophy, social studies, and psychology. I recall the time he postponed a test we were due to take; he'd seen how tired I was looking, and, when I told him I'd had to sit up the whole night to finish a story I was writing and hadn't had time to study for the test, he said, in front of the whole class:

"If one of your classmates has been writing a story, then I think we should put the test off for a couple of days."

As I approached the school fence, which seemed lower than before, as if colluding in my desire to get a better view of the place, I went on recalling my teachers. I could even see my history teacher, Mr. Adel Eid, the history teacher, who was as authentic as history itself. I recalled Mr. Yussef al-Azza, my English teacher, who was fair-haired like the English themselves. He spoke their language fluently, with a proper British accent, and taught it with great perfection. I remembered, too, the math teacher, Mr. Michel Rishmawi, who loved reading my stories as much as I hated mathematics. I asked him once to explain Einstein's theory of relativity, and have never forgotten how he summed it up.

"Imagine," he said, "waiting five minutes for your sweetheart to arrive. It would feel like five hours. Then imagine spending five hours with her—that would feel like spending five minutes."

A most satisfactory explanation of a theory not so easy to grasp!

I remembered, too, the school's principal, Ustadh[20] Amin, who devoted far more effort to culture at large than he did to education. I remembered Nazih Qoorah, as a teacher at Ramallah High School and a friend later on in Beirut. I recalled his sense of humor, the clever way he analyzed things, and his final move, when he surprised us all by deciding to go off to Tunis. It was there he died.

Like everyone else of my generation, I'd borrow books from the Ramallah Library—in accordance with Sartre's saying: "We are the semi-educated." Our generation was so serious about culture that we were enthusiastically devouring books borrowed from the Ramallah Library. We'd go to Ramallah's park to drink non-alcoholic beer, and to talk of our imagined projects, discuss Sartre, Naguib Mahfouz, Ghassan Kanafani, William Faulkner, as well as Harriet Beecher Stowe's *Uncle Tom's Cabin*. We'd discuss, too, Ahmad al-Shuqairi's last speech, which brought developments to a head, but only to help us back to where we should have been in the first place!

As we drank, Talaat would quote Toynbee, to the effect that the Palestinians were the worst advocates of the most just cause. We decided to publish a special issue of our magazine, devoted to the Palestinian cause—little knowing the decision would merely serve to put our magazine in the firing line.

I gave a start as I saw the name of Nazih Qoorah on a wall of the street where I entered the library, holding the membership card that had expired thirty years earlier and the copy of Richard Wright's *Uncle Tom's Children* that I'd borrowed on June 4, 1967,[21] and never had the chance to return. I'd never lost it, even so, in spite of all the places I'd been in and the countless other books I'd lost.

Slowly I placed the book in front of the librarian, who, as it happened, was the widow of the man after whom the street had been named.

"I'm sorry I'm so late returning this book, madam. I couldn't help it!"

"Oh, it doesn't matter. It's only thirty years!"

And so, after straying for thirty years, Uncle Tom's children returned at last—their faces, due to the suns of exile, a good deal darker than before—home to the library shelf where they'd once belonged, in the street that now bore the name of the martyr Nazih Qoorah. They'd returned after a war that broke out just one day after I'd borrowed the book, and sent them off far from home. I'd spent the whole night reading that book, meaning to return it the very next morning, on the fifth of June, 1967. The war, though, made me a matter of thirty years late!

～ 17 ～

The war of June 1967 wasn't the first Ramallah had seen. Tranquil and peaceful the town might have appeared, but it had never been sheltered from war. The Crusaders lived in Ramallah for a time, and the army of Ibrahim Pasha occupied it in 1834, as the Turkish army fought desperately to keep its last strongholds from falling to British occupation.

Ramallah had its own small wars too, like the one in the nineteenth century between the Qaisis and the Yemenis.[22] Red flags were hoisted on behalf of the Qaisis, white on behalf of the Yemenis. Battles took place in all the neighboring districts too, in what became known as the civil war. Since the people of Ramallah were mostly Qaisis, the town became a military headquarters from which daily operations were organized.

In fact the citizens of Ramallah weren't purely Qaisi. Some families were Yemeni by origin, like the Shaqra family, which could trace its ancestry back to Rashed al-Haddad's wife; she was from Bethlehem, and he'd married her after the death of his first wife, who'd died in Bethlehem on the way to Ramallah.

The odd thing is that, in normal times, both sides were eager to foster peaceful relations by showing respect for one another's traditions. A Qaisi bride, for instance, would dress in white when passing through a Yemeni quarter, a Yemeni bride in red if she passed through a Qaisi one.

There was another tussle in Ramallah, which came close to threatening its social peace. The town was divided into two distinctive groups, the Haddada, comprising the larger, more numerous tribe, and the Hamayel, to which all the other families belonged. In 1905, Ramallah witnessed the so-called Great Tumult. During the wedding ceremony of one of the Hamayel families, the bridal procession, on its way to church, had to pass through the Haddada quarter, and the songs from the procession so annoyed a drunken man from the Haddada that he tried to stop it passing through. This triggered a confrontation that began as a scuffle, graduated to the throwing of stones, and resulted, finally, in the firing of bullets. The riot flew almost out of control.

To avoid further escalation, and to put an end to a now full-scale battle spurred on by the shrieks of the women, a military force was called in from Jerusalem, and this succeeded in putting the chief agents behind bars.

Cooped up in a humid cell in Jerusalem, the men from the two groups had no option but to eat bread and salt together, which secured peace.[23] A historic peace treaty was subsequently signed at the headquarters of the Greek Orthodox Patriarchy, which had made strenuous efforts to have the men released.

Such minor clashes should not, though, be allowed to tarnish the glory of a great battle that took place in Ramallah. On the middle-class hill called Massyoun, where a new, luxurious quarter had spread over the previous few years, a fierce battle took place in March 1948, in which Ramallah contrived to deter the Jewish invasion and the ambitions of the Zionists.

A Jewish force from the Atarot Settlement, near Jerusalem Airport, attacked Massyoun, and a group of young armed men based in Ramallah succeeded in halting the attack and killing seventeen members of the invading force, after which the rest of the Jewish fighters turned back. None of the young men from Ramallah were killed.

Could it be, I wondered, that any of those who'd protected Masyoun and Ramallah from the Jewish assault were there still, living in those luxurious homes?

I stood on the hill of Massyoun, overlooking the Rafat road. It didn't need the eyes of Zarqa al-Yamama[24] to spot the later, ongoing Jewish advance. It was all too plain, in the form of those concrete jungles that were multiplying by the minute.

Would the people of Massyoun ever wake from their peaceful slumber, and see their home, protected once by the watchful eyes and zealous bullets of those young men of theirs, overwhelmed now with a strange onslaught of stone; see the steady advance of settlers who, in their greed, know no measure and no limit?

~ 18 ~

*A*ll the signs of inevitable war were casting their dark shadows on what remained of my generation. We thought, though, that it simply wouldn't happen; or, if it did, that Ramallah was bound to be unaffected. Abd al-Nasser was the war's sole target, and he alone, on behalf of the whole nation, would surely be proof against defeat.

But the war happened, on June 5, 1967, with no prior warning or consultation.

Like so many others, I listened to the radio as it broadcast the heroic illusions so soon to collapse. From the balcony of our home, overlooking al-Jamil Cinema, we watched the aircraft come crashing down from the skies above Jerusalem, supposing them to be just a few of the many shot-down enemy aircraft of which the radio constantly spoke.

On the second or third day of the war, those aircraft we thought the Arab forces had destroyed started bombarding

Ramallah. One of the bombs destroyed a factory for concrete blocks in al-Masayef Street, where I lived; the cement and rubble and sand from it filled the whole district with its debris, including the entrance of the building that was to be the last home I'd ever know in Ramallah.

The only human victim of this air raid, which filled the whole town with fear, was an old newspaper seller called Abul Habayeb. The aircraft had silenced him at last. He wouldn't wander the streets any more, shouting out those headlines proclaiming illusory victories and shot-down planes. It seemed, rather, as if those planes, still up there in the sky with their loads of black rancor, had hunted the echo of the old man's voice, bent on reducing it to silence.

Fortunate Abul Habayeb! He died a martyr along with his illusion. He didn't have to wake, to see the horrifying truth of that raid on the town, the planes appearing like a flock of dark ravens.

After Abul Habayeb's death, those with homes in the town center lived in constant fear of being killed, and a family friend, who lived in a nearby village, suggested to my father that we should leave our home, because the Jews were bound to focus their bombing on the heart of the town. My father, who'd known what it was to flee his home, hesitated. Then he said:

"I've left my home once. I'm not doing it again. It'll happen over my dead body!"

My mother, though, used her own special arts to persuade him. It would only, she said, be for a couple of days. Then the bombing would stop, and we could come back home. For my own part, I had nothing to say on the matter. It was my first experience of war.

As we took the rugged road to Ain Qinia, I could sense the mountains of the town we'd left behind shaking from the blasts of the bombs. Turning to look back, I saw the telegraph poles that had dotted the mountains all smashed and destroyed.

There, in that tranquil village nestling among the mountains, we were met by Abd al-Nasser's broken voice, which echoed the bleeding souls of the nation:

"We're accustomed to sharing good times and bad times alike—to sitting together—and to speaking the truth!"

The painful truth our leader told us so frankly, in an unsteady voice we'd never heard before, was that we'd been defeated. My mouth felt dry, my soul lost, as I tasted the bitter taste of defeat. And the pain only grew fiercer as I heard Abdel Halim sing:

Our village was washing her hair at the mouth of the stream
The day came when we couldn't pay her dowry.

The news broadcast announced the fall of Ramallah, and the enemy radio told people to hoist white flags. Amman radio, by contrast, urged the people to fight the enemy with nails and teeth.

My father insisted on returning home, and my mother showed no sign of disapproval.

"I'm going back to Ramallah," my father said. "I want to see what's happened. I'll check on our home—"

He walked alone, along a mountain road filled now with the check points of the invading army. He wouldn't let me go with him. In time of war, he said, young men were commonly arrested, even killed.

The very next day he trudged back to Ain Qinia, his eyes full of the bitter shock.

"We don't need to stay here," he said. "Ramallah and Ain Qinia have both been occupied. Get ready. We're going home!"

My mother asked him about the state of our home.

"It's all right," he answered. "It was hit by some bullets. They've broken the glass in some of the windows and torn the curtains."

He gazed at me.

"And their bullets tore the portrait of Abd al-Nasser," he said, his voice unsteady. "I picked up the pieces of glass," he added apologetically, "and got rid of the portrait."

My father went on saying for days how the enemy must surely have been targeting Abd al-Nasser, who lived in our home. How was it, otherwise, that their bullets hadn't broken the windows in any of the other homes in the block and smashed the pictures of their loved ones?

Now, for the first time in my life, I saw the invading forces, looking victorious with their heavy artillery, walking the streets of Ramallah. They occupied al-Manara Square and went around from street to street with their tanks. The people had a stunned air; there were so many questions unanswered, so many facts unclear. It wasn't possible to understand, to imagine even, just what had happened.

Ramallah had entered the occupation era. The lighthouse, where all the dreams, all the lovers and the demonstrators had once met, had a mournful air that day. The water had even stopped gushing from the mouths of the stone lions. The Israeli military jeeps, loudspeakers blaring, called on people to bring their weapons to the lighthouse and throw them down there.

The first days of the occupation were slow, filled with doubt and expectation. The people were busy picking up the pieces of what remained of their lives and homes, and checking on friends and members of their families.

I was deeply worried about my friend Yasser, and made constant inquiries about him, especially after I heard that the village of Yalo, where he was spending his summer holiday, had been totally destroyed. There were stories of young men being rounded up and killed in Yalo, Imwas, and Beit Nouba, the three villages sited on the green line where the *fedayeen*[25] crossed late at night to lighten our days.

The one happy moment I recall amid the utter misery of those days was when I heard a tap on the door and opened— and there was my friend Yasser. The questions came pouring out, from our eyes and lips, with a bitterness and a distress we'd never known before.

He had the air of one bearing a heavy burden: of a long journey and the heritage of our roving ancestors, who'd crossed the burning moving sands of a desert unknown to maps.

We embraced, as we'd never done before. And we wept as we'd never done before, and never would again.

"Aunt—aunt—what are you doing?"
"Waiting!"
After a few days, people began celebrating the reunion with their loved ones, who'd come to visit them from the Palestine occupied in 1948. They'd given up the wait for the Arab armies to make their dream of liberation come true.

My aunt was the one person left in al-Bireh who still nourished her dreams and impossible desires. There she sat on the balcony, waiting for the return of her loved one who'd gone away twenty years before.

"Aunt—aunt—what are you waiting for?"

"I'm waiting for your uncle Ali, Abu Ibrahim. If only he'd come back one day. Even if he was married to a Jewish girl!"

I wished, too, that he'd come back one day. He'd gone off to al-Muzairia'a, in 1948, to bring some of my aunt's cherished things from their home; he'd never returned. Would the occupation bring my aunt, at last, the happiness she'd lost two decades before?

But no, my aunt never celebrated her husband's return. Not even when al-Bireh had been occupied for ten years.

She visited me one day in Beirut, all hope lost, at last, of her husband's return. She'd come, she told me, to say goodbye. She was sure she'd finally see her husband again in heaven. Perhaps he was sitting on his balcony in the next world, waiting for her. She thanked God, she said (smiling, the happiness clear in her eyes) that he'd never come back to her with a Jewish girl.

"Aunt—how old are you?"

"How am I to know, son? Get a pen and a piece of paper, and start adding it up. I lived eleven years under Turkish rule, thirty-one years under the British mandate, nineteen years under the Jordanian regime, eleven years under the Jewish occupation. Add all those together."

I added up all those years my aunt had lived, under the various regimes. Then it struck me. The name of Palestine had never been mentioned.

My aunt said goodbye to me and hurried back to al-Bireh. And there she died soon after, going off to meet the husband waiting for her on a balcony far more beautiful than her own in al-Bireh.

When I left the Palestinian Parliament, the chair was still there on the balcony of the building opposite. Once the preserve of my aunt, it was consigned to oblivion now.

After a few days of occupation, the open, friendly father who'd never minded us sharing his pack of cigarettes, and drinking alcohol, and every so often talking about women, changed totally. He started issuing military-style orders, the first of them addressed to me:

"You're to leave Ramallah at once. I've arranged for you to cross the bridge with our neighbors, who have American passports. You've three missions to carry out: to send us news about Suleiman"—this was my soldier brother at camp in the Khalil [Hebron] mountains—"to send news to your brothers in Kuwait, and to get your high school certificate. We don't want to see you back here for a year. Don't come back without your high school certificate."

When I left Ramallah, I thought I'd be coming back in a few months. There was no chance of that!

Some months later, I was standing on the balcony of my apartment in Mustafa Ramadan Yussef Street in Alexandria, watching the falling rain and the sea waves that found their way into my memories, stirring up all the nostalgic feelings inside me. The rain was heavy, the sea waves were high; but somehow the rain looked different. There'd be no rain like the rain of Ramallah.

~ 19 ~

*R*ain like no other rain. Ramallah's streets quivered in the heavy rain pouring down from a sky filled with dark secrets. It was as though the rain was refurbishing the town with homes washed clean, as though the stones had refound their lost glory, the earth its color of ground coffee.

In all the cities of my long exile, I never stopped searching for rain like that of Ramallah.

From Alexandria to Amman, where I'd gaze from my window at the trees surrounding the Sports City, where I'd watch the rain falling gently, but never feeling like the rain of Ramallah. I'd hold the trembling hand of my love, and we'd walk through the rain of the misty street, amid the pine trees at the University of Jordan. But the rain never felt like the rain of Ramallah.

Once more I found myself far away, overlooking the blue sea, with its tide closing in from the depth of the unknown, the unreachable horizons. I'd stand on the balcony, watching the rain as it fell on the sea of Beirut, and on the city's peerless cedars. The rain felt warm from the gunpowder burning the city. But still it wasn't like the rain of Ramallah.

I recall how, once, my love and I were caught in the rain in Souk El Ghareb. Hand in hand, we raced through streets that were awash, and along the wet sidewalks, keeping one another warm with our burning desire. Then, suddenly, the rain stopped. It was summer rain. Happy in what seemed to us like a dream, we moved on—

I searched for that rain in all the capitals, and in remote villages not even to be found on maps, but I never found any rain like the rain of Ramallah.

Rain like no other rain!

Ramallah had its own thunder, its own lightning and rain. There I climbed to the heavens on those threads of rain. I heard Ramallah's thunder, and I recalled the old women's tales. The thunder, they'd say, was just the holy echo of the hooves of two white winged horses, the horses of Abraham and St. George, who'd chosen, from the seven skies created by God, to ride the skies of Ramallah.

It would have been pointless to ask the people of Ramallah how they came to fashion that story. Rather, we'd have to ask the Creator Himself, who chose the sky of Ramallah from which to send down such rain, making that sky an open meadow for the wind and for the horses bearing prophets and saints. Ramallah was created for the sky of the gods' chariots!

I was coming to terms with my nostalgia, and with a ceaseless bleeding that sprang from a longing with no end.

Still, the rain made me long all the more for Ramallah. And longing would not be tempered, or assuaged, by a visit!

⁓

Rain like no other rain. Rain that restored the spirit in aging hearts.

I fled the quivering streets, seeking out that lonely, dismal room in the small hotel. There, looking from the east window, I watched the rainfall, saw how a naked fig tree quivered under the rain, with its blossoms trying hard to release themselves from the bark worn by the tree branches. At the base of the trunk was a spread of early green grass, herald of a coming green spring with its swathes of narcissus. Behind the tree stood an old brick house, not unlike my first home. The familiar sight set my heart afire, and the pouring rain washed away my memory.

As I reached out to touch the rain, from behind the iron bars of the window, my heart broke from all the pain and sorrow I'd endured over the years. I listened to my own heavy breathing and that of the rain, felt the fire flaring up in my spirit, igniting my feeling of nostalgia. Ramallah looked gloomy, and I looked old; but my longing for the town and the rain would never fade.

Rain like no other rain—

Three decades on, the faint sound from neighboring al-Bardawni brought back to me the sorrow in the sound of raindrops, and in the sound, like weeping, of the gushing drains, in harmony with the grieving in my heart.

There swept through me, suddenly, a sense of being lonely and abandoned in the wilderness. The whole mass of my memories was flashing through me there, before the window of that small, cold hotel room, where, through the iron bars, I gazed at what appeared to be my homeland, and where I watched the rain that looked like no other rain.

Looking from the window of a small hotel, it seemed to me I'd never known a bed, never known wild dreams, or possessed a home, where the town's stones and its people weren't alive, already, in my heart!

A hotel! All those years, all that longing—and here I found myself, come back to a hotel room. My heart was plunged in a rain of its own. I wept till the dawn came.

Here I was at last, coming out from my written text, entering the town to roam its streets and alleys. Here I was, complying with all the rules for entry, rules that blocked a road engraved so deep in my memory. You couldn't get to Ramallah without passing along that road, and glimpsing Jerusalem with its gold and silver domes, and the sunlight dancing on its walls and markets and graveyards.

Here was Ramallah at last, looking just as my heart had always pictured it. I'd returned, finally, to the place, but the place hadn't returned to me. And so I'd searched for what once had been, for what had been lost—

A young man—longing forever—and cherishing forever.

The End

Notes

1 Al-Mutanabbi (916–966) is one of the greatest poets of the Arabic language. Muhyi al-Din Ibn 'Arabi (1165–1240) is one of the greatest Islamic mystics (sufis) and a poet of great human sensitivity who believed in the unity of the universe and of human love and experience.

2 This book was written following two visits to Ramallah. The first was at the beginning of 1995, the second at the end of 1996—that is, before and after the deployment of Israeli occupation forces around the Palestinian towns. [Author's note]

3 *Marhaba* has come to be known internationally as an Arabic word of welcome, its root, *rahiba*, alluding at once to space and welcome.

4 The Iraqi Badr Shakir al-Sayyab (1926–1964) was a seminal figure in the development of modern Arabic poetry. His famous poem "Rain Song" highlighted the potential for the use of myth in poetry.

5 The smallest coin in the Palestinian currency was the mellim. Ten mellims made a piaster.

6 *The Thief and the Dogs* is a famous novel by the Nobel Prize–winning Egyptian novelist Naguib Mahfouz (1911–2006), in which Said Mahran, the thief of the title, is both antihero and victim.

7 A traditional entertainment like a magic lantern show, highly popular with children of this period.

8 Fareq Warrad was a Communist who was nevertheless popular with nationalists, being, like most Communists of the time, supportive of Nasser.

9 This was a highly popular radio station run by Egypt and dedicated to the political situation of the Arab world.

10 A famous Egyptian singer at the time.

11 An old Arab habit stipulated that the bearer of good tidings and often also, as is the case above, a person present, expect something of a reward or present.

12 This means "permission," often said as a signal of arrival usually of a male stranger alerting the women of the house to either cover up or disappear.

13 Shammout (d. 2006) is one of Palestine's major painters, who dedicated his work to painting the modern history and tragedy of the Palestinians.

14 One of the four Orthodox Caliphs who ruled after the Prophet's death. He has come down in history as one of the most righteous and firm rulers in Arab history. He was assassinated in 643AD.

15 He is alluding here to the year when the democratic government of Nabulsi was dismissed, as stated above.

16 The historian Aref al-Aref (1892–1973) wrote extensively on the Palestine Disaster of 1948 and its aftermath. He was specifically noteworthy for the minute and painstaking care with which he recorded individual loss, such as the death or imprisonment of particular persons and the demolition of particular homes.

17 The British soldier John Glubb, commonly known as Glubb Pasha, was an influential military figure in Jordan until his dismissal in 1956.

18 *Nargila*: A kind of pipe in which the tobacco is drawn through water.

19 The poetry of the Syrian Nizar Qabbani (1923–1998) is immensely popular throughout the Arab world. Many of his poems deal exuberantly with the subject of love.

20 A word put before the first or second name, usually of a cultured person, implying respect and appreciation. The same word would also mean a teacher. Here the two meanings are combined.

21 i.e., one day before the chaos and deep distress of the 1967 June War and the colossal shock it dealt to the rising generation of Arabs all over the Arab world, particularly the Palestinians.

22 The enmity between the two major divisions of the old Arabs, since pre-Islamic times, into Yemenis, who hailed mostly from Yemen, and Qaisis, who constituted the rest, has been at the root of much strife and bloodshed in Arab medieval history. To find out here that it had persisted to quasi-modern times is shockingly interesting. [Editor's note]

23 Sharing food, here designated as eating bread and salt together,

meant the security of peace and friendship. This is an old Arab habit that exists up till now, particularly in traditional quarters.

24 Zarqa al-Yamama was a legendary Arab figure able to see, in the far distance, things invisible to others.

25 *Fedayeen* are freedom fighters sworn to fight and redeem their country with their blood. The root of the word is *fada* ("redeemed with his life").